PULP
Literature

PULP Literature

PULP LITERATURE PRESS

Issue No. 32, Autumn 2021

Publisher: Pulp Literature Press; Managing Editor: Jennifer Landels; Senior Editor: Mel Anastasiou; Acquisitions Editor: Genevieve Wynand; Poetry Editors: Daniel Cowper & Emily Osborne; Assistant Editors: Samantha Olson, Brooklynn Hook, Veronika Kos, Melisa Gruger; Copy Editors: Amanda Bidnall, Mary Rykov; Proofreaders: Mary Rykov and Genevieve Wynand; Graphic Design: Amanda Bidnall; Cover Design: Kate Landels; First Readers: Carol McCauley, Jessica Fabrizius, Jeya Thiessen; Subscriptions: Carol McCauley; Advertising: Samantha Olson. For advertising rates, direct inquiries to info@pulpliterature.com.

Cover painting, *The Pianist Who Serenaded the Mermaids with Chopin's Nocturne in E Minor* by Tais Teng. Artwork for 'Houses' by Matthew Nielsen. All other illustrations by Mel Anastasiou.

Pulp Literature: ISSN 2292-2164 (Print), ISSN 2292-2172 (Digital), Issue No. 32, Autumn 2021.

Published quarterly by Pulp Literature Press, 21955 16 Ave, Langley, BC, Canada V2Z 1K5, pulpliterature.com, at $15.00 per copy. Annual subscription $50.00 in Canada, $68.00 in continental USA, $86.00 elsewhere. Printed in Victoria, BC, Canada, by First Choice Books / Victoria Bindery. Copyright © 2021 Pulp Literature Press. All stories and works of art copyright © 2021 their authors as per bylines.

Pulp Literature Press gratefully acknowledges the support of the Canada Council for the Arts.

Pulp Literature is a proud member of the Magazine Association of BC and Magazines Canada.

TABLE OF CONTENTS

From the Pulp Lit Pulpit
Of Pulp and Pumpkins — 7

Crossroads
Dan MacIsaac — 11

Feature Interview
Dan MacIsaac — 25

Ghost Walking
Mel Anastasiou — 31

Just Another Date Night on the Highway Out of Town
Zandra Renwick — 55

Come Back Around
Sarina Bosco — 69

Solstice
Melissa Nelson — 79

The Canadian Invasion
David Perlmutter — 83

Cold Blessing
Kelsey Hutton — 97

Attempted Murder
Leslie Wibberley
111

SiWC Storyteller's Award
Robin Malcolm
127

The Magpie Award for Poetry
Frances Boyle, David Barrick, Aldona Dziedziejko
145

Houses, Part II
Matthew Nielsen
157

The Shepherdess: Intrigue
JM Landels
173

The Pianist Who Serenaded the Mermaids with Chopin's Nocturne in E Minor
Tais Teng
201

FROM THE PULP LIT PULPIT

Of Pulp and Pumpkins

Ah, autumn, we're ready for you. Ready for the cooling air, the glowing sunlight, the brilliant red and orange leaves, the noisy geese in their southward-bound vees. And, of course, for the pumpkins.

While the cafés fill with the heady scent of spiced lattes, the pumpkins wait. They wait in fields and grocery stores and farmers' markets. They wait for the carvers, Michelangelos all, to test their heft, scrutinize their surfaces, and imagine the possibilities. To paraphrase the master, the carvers see the face in the gourd and will carve until they set it free. Freed not as *David*s in white marble, but as jack-o'-lanterns in orange flesh.

Yes, orange might be the preferred Jack, but out beyond the ubiquitous cardboard bins exists a veritable pumpkin rainbow: red, yellow, green, blue, grey, black, white, blush, and brown. And not just round and smooth, but squat, slumped, stout, knobby, pocked, goose-necked, deep-ridged, pear-shaped, palm-sized, and wagon worthy.

And such fantastic names! Batwing, Baby Boo, Cotton Candy, Goosebumps, Harvest Moon, Jack-Be-Little, Jack-B-Quick, Knucklehead, Long Island Cheese, Magic Lantern, Moonshine, Scheherazade, Snack Jack, Super Moon, Speckled Hound, Sweetie Pie, Warty Goblin. And, the best to end this endless list: One Too Many.

Here at *Pulp Literature*, we delight in bringing you a cross-genre cornucopia of literary cucurbits. Stories and poems of many shapes and sizes, tastes and textures, all have a home in the *Pulp Lit* pumpkin patch. And what a bounty it is! So set down the carving knife, pick up a spiced latte or hot chocolate or apple cider, and spend a little time with us.

~ *Genevieve Wynand*

ɪɴ ᴛʜɪs ɪssᴜᴇ
We begin oceanside with cover artist **Tais Teng**, and a lonely piano on a blustery beach inviting us to uncover the many stories of this issue, including one by the artist himself: 'The Pianist Who Serenaded the Mermaids with Chopin's Nocturne in E Minor'.

Carved by the Pacific, three faces of the West Coast emerge in three historical moments: 'Crossroads' by feature author **Dan MacIsaac**, 'Ghost Walking' by **Mel Anastasiou**, and the SiWC Storyteller's Award winner 'My Name is Philomena' by **Robin Malcolm**.

David Perlmutter, in 'Canadian Invasion', takes us on a cross-Canada tour. Keep an eye out for those semaphores, eh? And in 'The Shepherdess: Intrigue' by **JM Landels**, Toinette navigates the complexities of the court of Versailles. Mind your manners with the Queen, *s'il vous plaît*.

Whether it's a greasy slice of pizza or a kill from the hunt, 'Just Another Date Night on the Highway out of Town' by

Zandra Renwick and 'Come Back Around' by **Sarina Bosco** prove it's rarely a good sign when your dinner starts talking.

Parents face their demons in 'Attempted Murder' by **Leslie Wibberly** and 'Cold Blessing' by **Kelsey Hutton**. And the finale of **Matthew Nielsen**'s 'Houses' illustrates the importance of owning—and sharing—your story.

The Magpie Award for Poetry winner and runners-up, **Frances Boyle, David Barrick,** and **Aldona Dziedziejko,** spin gritty memories, childhood dreams, and a mouthful of metaphors with their stunning poetry. And a young woman yearning for exploration leads us to dream of the future in **Melissa Nelson**'s Hummingbird Prize runner-up, 'Solstice'.

CROSSROADS

Dan MacIsaac

Dan MacIsaac *writes from Metchosin, BC. His short stories have appeared in many journals in the UK, Canada, and the US, including* Stand, The Dalhousie Review, Grain, *and* The New Quarterly. *His fiction was short-listed for the CBC Short Story Prize. Brick Books published his poetry collection,* Cries from the Ark. *His website is danmacisaac.com.*

Crossroads

In 1925, people hustled to keep up with all the mudslinging and muckraking. And everybody up and down the Valley was quick to pass that dirt on to the next keen listener. No wonder the whole Valley figured they knew all about Marta Toth playing around. That kind of woman wouldn't stay penned up in the woods between the mountains and the sea. In the beer parlour, some of the boozers called her the town pump. Though they didn't dare mouth that slur when her man, the slope-shouldered, lug-knuckled logger, Adam Wainwright, was within earshot, downing a lager, boot heels hooked onto the brass foot rail. Sure, he'd never churched her and she'd never had a child by him. Still, people hissed that she was a cheater all the same. They all just knew Adam had no clue about Marta's flings. But not even the most hopped-up Comox Valley tattler had the gumption to tip him off. They'd all hush around Adam——when he'd stride by the open window of Tilly's Tea Shoppe, where the finest townie matrons huddled around the lacy tables; or when in the Quarterway he'd shove his way up to the bar top cluttered with beefy elbows and clunky beer glasses.

By noon of the day after Marta first showed up on the public dock, she'd been garlanded with fibs and perjuries by the scandalmongers in the Valley. The busybodies figured they had all they needed to learn about the new arrival on the night ferry. The scuttlebutt had come right out of the crooked mouth of Merle Bartram, the docker. Bartram had the whole morning to rouse the most notorious tongue-waggers, and they'd stuffed a bug-swarm of lies into the town's collective ear that the logger, on leave from camp, had crossed over to the Mainland to go on a tear. They eagerly passed on the sworn confidence from the dockhand about how Adam had let slip he'd met the young woman turning tricks in Gastown and had talked her into keeping house for him instead of keeping bad company. Adam had paid her ferry ticket, plunked her down in his buckboard, and hauled her up to his cabin by the crossroads.

Knowing that the logger had a woman now, not one gossiper was surprised to see Adam in the late afternoon stride across the creaky stoop crowded with ne'er-do-wells slouching outside Proctor's General Store. With a woman—any kind of woman—in the home, he'd need to pick up supplies. Adam pressed through that bunch of loafers and dawdlers, not saying a word.

The Valley never heard the honest-to-god truth—that Marta only turned mattresses for a living. Backbreaking hours she worked as a chambermaid in the Castle Hotel. That Granville Street establishment was where Adam had been staying while he scouted around the city for a lightly-used McLaughlin touring car that had an engine he could tinker with. He was a saver but not a cheapskate, frugal but also forward-looking. He had money in his pocket to spend on the right vehicle for the right price. It made no sense to keep hitching horseflesh to a buckboard if you wanted to get somewhere in good time.

Unlike most everybody from the Valley, Adam minded his own beeswax; and his contact with the bustling chambermaid would have stayed at just a swap of nods in the top floor hall. But he almost tripped over her as he was heading out the back way from the hotel to stretch his legs before bed. He didn't like crowds, so he'd avoided the lobby exit. There was a lot of kerfuffle outside on Granville Street, with an unruly audience flooding out of the Orpheum Theatre after the late show. On the rough cement right outside the rear door of the hotel lay the chambermaid, kinked like a spot prawn. A thuggish man in a torn shirt leaned over the woman, stumbled back, then lurched forward, spewing a cataract of obscenities.

The logger reached out and up to grasp the thug's massive left shoulder.

"Bugger off," snarled the brute, eyes flat and hard as rivets. And he broke the woodsman's grip by heaving sideways and smacking the heel of his right hand like a mallet against Adam's outstretched arm. The thug wheeled back around and Adam heard the thud of boot to flesh, along with, "Dirty bitch."

Adam cocked both fists and hit the drunk hard with his left then his right on that horseshoe jaw. But the big man didn't drop. He lunged, bringing up burly arms to grapple with Adam, then released the hold, thrusting meaty hands inside to grab the logger's throat. Adam cannoned a knee into his attacker's groin, but the man only grunted as though he'd been gelded and there was nothing there to hammer on. As his air choked off, Adam's chest heaved and his vision greyed. The woman uncoiled and, with a stamping kick, clobbered the thug's ankle bone. He sagged but kept his death grip around Adam's windpipe. She kicked at his other ankle, striking it with the heel of her sturdy work shoe.

The brute toppled backward and yanked Adam with him. The logger landed hard on top, his weight slamming the back of the thug's skull on the cement.

Adam levered up, coughing. He wobbled to the door frame and hung on while his head and airway cleared. Their attacker lay still like a stone slab.

The chambermaid rose to her knees on the stained cement. Her dark eyes flashed. "He's not near dead. Got a head like an anvil."

Adam pointed shakily behind him and said, "Maybe get back inta the hotel and report this."

The chambermaid stood up. Like a poplar, she was slender and tall—tall enough to look Adam straight in the eye. She tossed her head, curls like catkins spiralling on to her shoulders. She'd have none of that. Her shift was over and the hotelier didn't look kindly on what he called shenanigans. Cupping a hand over a bashed cheek, the maid told Adam that the man lying prone was her husband and that booze made him wildly jealous about her working nights, when all she did was mop out the hotel restaurant for the extra pay that he'd guzzle down. It wasn't the first time he'd shown up guttered at the end of her late shift and laid a beating on her. One of these times, she said, he'd beat the living daylights out of her. So she wasn't going home anytime soon.

"How 'bout I put you up, not at the Castle?" Adam offered.

The chambermaid hummed and hawed awhile.

He added, "It coulda gone bad."

With a fingertip, she touched the ridge of her hurt cheekbone. "For both of us. But I'm more used to it. So maybe you owe me enough."

She looked him up and down. "You're too roughed up to be trouble. And no friend's up and about at this hour. Wouldn't want to rouse one. So all right. I know a cheap hotel on Seymour."

Hobbling along the alley, Adam asked, "How's the cheek?"

The chambermaid shrugged and eyed his throat. "Those thumb prints look like love bites. Better put on a high collar for a while."

He chuckled, which sent shards of pain along his gullet.

Adam saw her to her room then walked gingerly back to the Castle, sticking to the lit streets. He opened the hotel door to the alley and peered out. No sign of the woman's husband. Adam checked out of the hotel and carried his canvas kit bag down to Howe Street. He took a room across the hall from Marta's. She didn't seem at all surprised when he knocked on her door in the morning. They ended up sharing a room and bed until the end of his leave. Adam never did find a touring car.

Day before he was due back, Adam started his pitch. "I know you're married and all, but——"

She broke in, "I'm a one-man woman." She folded her arms. Warding him off? he wondered. Adam didn't know what to say. He stalled. He stared.

She gave a tight smile, not showing any teeth. "One man at a time."

"All right," he said.

She unfolded her arms and reached out to grasp his hand, squeezing. "You know, he's out there."

He could feel the calluses on her palm, rough as husks. "All right," he repeated.

"But it's like he's dead——to me."

So they decided that Marta would rush home for her clothes while her ironworker husband had a shift on the bridge. And she'd come over with Adam to the Island to try out the cabin in the Valley. She'd have a fresh start away from the lout.

But there's always another lout lurking about. Merle Bartram, off work, was killing time with a quarter bottle of rye down by the docks when Marta, tall and head held high, carpetbag in her right hand, strolled off the CPR night ferry from Vancouver in a late spit of rain. He would have wolf-whistled if lanky Adam Wainwright hadn't been loping along beside her under the dock lights and hovering a battered umbrella over her head as they headed up to the livery. She was a looker, in spite of the yellowing of an old bruise on her cheek where the powder had dripped off. Windborne rain had lashed her during the crossing when she'd been out on deck.

Six months back, Bartram and a crew of boom-rats had bested Adam and a couple of camp swampers in a bar-room brawl. In the Valley, there was no love lost between dockers and loggers. Lumbermen considered longshoremen a bunch of numbskulled slackers, while dockworkers thought lumberjacks were jackasses — puffed up and overpaid ones. But Bartram figured Adam didn't hold that shellacking against him. Much. Though Bartram had upped a wrangle over a billiards game into a donnybrook. That night, wharfies had woodsmen outnumbered by far. Bartram had liked those odds, and it was a breeze for him to get the crew riled up. Though Bartram was a big two-fisted man, he much preferred to get a mob fired up and stay out of the fray himself. Indeed, he dove under the nearest table when the chairs and glasses started flying in that ruction.

Bartram called out to the logger from the shadows, maybe a dozen feet away from the couple. The greeting had a smart-ass twang to it.

"Evenin', Wainwright."

Adam walked on, wordless.

Bartram hooted, "Not your sister, I bet."

Adam said nothing, but the dockhand could tell the lumberjack heard him by the sudden hitch in his step and the stiffening of his neck as he resisted turning his head toward the caller. Bartram gnawed the inside of his cheek. That girl looked too pricey for Adam — and more than a woodchopper deserved. The docker downed the rest of the bottle and tossed it, shattering the empty against a tarred piling.

The nosy parkers in the Valley were already wary of Adam. He was an oddball. A faller out of camp ought to have cleared off all the trees on his land and turned it into a stump farm where you could at least graze a few head of cattle.

Not Adam. He didn't even call his property a timber lot. He had knocked down only enough firs and cedars in his small forest to build himself a squat log cabin and a narrow stable in a clearing beneath a low bluff. Along the crossroads, his trees loomed in a herringbone pattern like Harris Tweed. He'd punched in an access road that snaked through a maze of broad trunks. Marta and he rolled down that road in his creaky wagon, and she took up housekeeping in the cabin. Adam kept the curvy driveway clean and smooth. No windfall or potholes. "Easy in. Easy out," he told Marta, leaving her the buckboard and sorrel mare when he left for camp, hiking out to the crossroads to catch a ride on the company crummy. But she didn't leave the place much, walled in behind all that wood.

Marta mostly stuck to the property ever since her first Saturday alone in town. At Proctor's, she had circled giddily through the store, choosing supplies. Up at the counter, the hammerheaded proprietor told her that he could take her order but she couldn't walk out with any goods until he heard from Adam. She blushed to a peony pink and bit her tongue. Hangers-on snickered.

She got even more skittish because of her next visit into town on another Saturday a couple of months later. While she was walking past a boarded-up storefront, that longshoreman Merle Bartram reached out and grabbed hold of her wrist. The docker was built like a pile driver. But he was three sheets to the wind, so she was able to shake him off by mule-kicking him in the knee. Heart and head pounding, she rushed to the buckboard. The longshoreman, clutching his leg, yelled a string of curses long as a trolling line.

Bartram staggered back to the tavern where he wrapped rope-callused fingers around a cold beer and griped about her. The more he drank, the more slander he spouted. He reminded his listeners how he'd known at first sight she was a streetwalker by the way she swung her hips, sashaying through the rain, and that Adam just figured he'd reform her——ha! Then he told another cock and bull story about how, a few days after she landed ashore, she flounced into town and followed, no, led him into a blind alley where she jumped at him and he had her like stew meat on a spit. The docker raised his free hand and slammed that rope-roughened fist on the sodden tabletop, making the amber glasses jump. His scurrilous tale was followed by bleary and fantastic eyewitness accounts by his fellow boozehounds about riffraff seen slipping along the shady way to and from her cabin bed and her driving Adam's buckboard down the backroads, looking for any randy lad. At last call, God's truth sworn on an empty bottle of rye was that she was a genuine Jezebel, faithful only to being faithless. Solemn hoppy oaths were slurred that whenever Adam was away she played the field. She'd been two-timing the woodsman times twenty. Blowhard bar talk, taken home to the wives, turned into malicious pillow talk. Catty bedroom chat became fact, ironclad as a stovetop kettle.

Cruel falsehoods circulated through the Valley for a good year. Then, come August, in the middle of a heatwave, Marta took the wagon down into town to buy a block of glacier ice at Proctor's, as Adam was due back from camp the next day. Bartram, who'd been making a beeline for the bar, stopped to watch her wrestle a crate of ice onto the buckboard. She gave the crate a good heave, then strapped it on.

Oh, she's a wiry one, thought Bartram. The dockhand kept his distance. He remembered how she had nearly crushed his kneecap. He'd kept quiet about that.

Bartram had already drained a flask back in the rooming house. The more booze in him, the more he got riled. Her show of routine grit irked him. Over the drinking hours in the beer parlour, he yammered himself and a small posse into a frenzy. At last call, the bunch boiled out of the tavern. They crammed into a couple of carriages, picking up some hooch at a speakeasy. Flung out at the crossroads, the empties smashed on hardpan. The rabble tilted and pitched down the access road, and stumbled, hollering, around the cabin. But the low-set building stayed dark and silent even when the drunken gang hammered on the heavy door until the hinges juddered.

Marta crept out of bed and crouched beside the pulsing door, clutching an iron poker. She'd put up a fight, make grown men groan. But the door had been stoutly built — double-planked with Doug fir and brass butt hinges screwed tight into an oak frame. It did not give way.

When Adam returned, she said nothing about the ordeal. But during his furlough, he may have caught wind of the tale or some twisted version of it. He liked to chug a beer or two, and there were only four taverns in the Valley. But he never spoke to her about any gossipy goings-on nor recounted loose talk.

The day before Adam headed back to camp, he was out on the porch, stooped over one of his work boots and greasing the leather tongue, the welt stitches, and the back seam with brisk fingers.

Marta placed a slim, hard hand on his sloped shoulder. "This spell—think it'll hold?"

He shrugged. She squeezed his shoulder, feeling the thick ridge of muscle. He returned to the task at hand, slathering lardy oil around the eyeholes. She went back inside and leaned against the sink full of suds.

He came back in and stood beside her. "Too much a this, and they'll close up camp. Woods turn inta a tinderbox."

Gently, he bumped his hip against hers and dropped his oily fingers into the soapy water, swishing. "Greasin' my boots for luck. Bring on the rain."

That night, she could smell a hint of grease still on his fingers as they tangled in her hair. And there was an oily glide as his hands moved over the soft skin of her throat. She wanted his body to cut into hers like a whipsaw. She wanted that again on waking, but he had left in the early hours for the logging camp in a sputter of rain.

As she lay there under a bare sheet, quilt tossed off in the night, she wished he were still stretched out beside her. She wondered if she should tell Adam when he got out of camp that they were good together, better than married. Though she had shown him that. But why should she think of speaking up? He never said much, and, being with him, she'd taken up the habit of being tight-lipped. Matching him.

In camp, Adam was the jack-of-all-trades as well as a faller. He could fix almost anything. Any busted thing. Even mend an arm—once he'd splinted a high rigger's fractured arm after the man had tumbled off a treetop. Even fix breakfast, they'd joke in camp, 'cause he'd flip some high fluffy flapjacks for the crew whenever the cook took ill from homebrew or took off bushed. But Adam couldn't fix himself when the topside of an old growth spruce crashed down on his leg, crushing it, and he bled out. The boys hauled him out on a springboard. They stowed the body in the railway depot, the undertaker being out visiting family down island.

The bullheaded foreman hopped into his Model T Highboy and drove up under an overcast sky to break the news to Marta. Meanwhile, a knot of Valley dwellers gathered outside the depot. The little black Ford rattled back into the railyard. Marta got out, bleak-faced. Her sleeveless dress was creased, and she was without coat or hat. Trailing after the foreman, Marta walked stiffly through the main door of the depot and stayed inside a good quarter hour. She came out blinking. Her lower lip quivered as the women stepped toward her, murmuring. The men just scuffed their boots against the ground, kicking at dirt clods and litter. One gent gulped, his Adam's apple wrinkled like a walnut. Another cracked his joints from knuckles to neck. Marta suddenly wailed. Hunched and shawled, the Valley women, who'd shunned her before, gathered around her, shushing and soothing. Marta left off keening, and her sinewy arms dropped to her sides. White and hard as branches stripped of bark, those limbs did not tremble.

After a good while, Marta spoke in a dry, halting voice, "He musta heard. About the trouble this last time. And out there worrying over me—let his guard down."

More shushing and soothing came from the ladies like the buzzing of honeybees on the comb, though Marta wasn't crying. Most of those women knew a confession when they heard one. But they pretended to be oblivious. Made in the open air, it was too sudden, too stark, too blameworthy. They stuck to consoling. The Valley women took turns trying to comfort Marta, one or two of them secretly fretting over how with her man gone there'd be nobody to hold back the hussy now. The kindest busybody patted the stricken girl's fingers, which were pale but rough like poorly rinsed roots, and considered who in time might be just the right bachelor fella to take on Marta. Somebody homely and not too picky.

All the Valley men stood back. Now and then a few of them would each steal a look at Merle Bartram, who was leaning against the depot wall, big arms folded like a railway crossing sign. Three of those onlookers had run with the pack lurching up to the cabin while the man of the house was away. Liquored up and blundering by cloud-shrouded night, they'd reeled both ways through Adam's dark woods. Each had thought himself wild and adventuresome at the time. Not sneaks. Not just aiming to steal in and out of a bed. They were rowdy boys eager to raise a ruction. Each had justified that a woman like her couldn't rightly say no, couldn't rightly be a one-man woman.

The Valley men—gawky sons, lazy-eyed bachelors, sly husbands—the lot of them stood back. They all thought of the man taken by ill fortune as they stared at Marta—she gone almost gaunt. And they realized there could be no question now. Not one of them had any claim on her. As they saw it, she belonged to the dead.

FEATURE INTERVIEW

Dan MacIsaac

Pulp Literature: *'Crossroads' takes place in a 1920s-era logging town on Vancouver Island. Could you tell us about the inspiration for the story, and how Marta and Adam came to be?*

Dan MacIsaac: Growing up in Nanaimo, I listened carefully whenever older relatives talked about what it was like 'back then' on the Island. Although the atmosphere of 'Crossroads' emerges from Island memories, the plot and characters are inventions.

Beginning with memory, a writer can aspire to make something authentic and new. The mother of the Muses was Memory, the Greek goddess Mnemosyne.

PL: *With 'Crossroads' you venture outside of poetry and into the world of short story. Did you make any interesting discoveries along the way? How, for you, does each form inform the other?*

DM: I have always written in both forms — which cross-pollinate. They enhance each other. Poetry teaches us to focus, to avoid the extraneous. Short fiction highlights pace and, particularly for narrative poetry, points out the arc of plot and the centrality of conflict. The common quality that I value most in both literary forms is lyricism.

PL: *In your poetry collection* Cries from the Ark, *we meet creatures great and small and encounter humankind's place within, and displacement of, the natural world. Do you believe we are at a point of no return, or is there reason to hope?*

DM: There is reason to hope because people are speaking up and taking action to protect the planet. Climate change and endangered ecosystems are getting meaningful attention. Here in BC, we have conservation organizations such as the BC Parks Foundation and Habitat Acquisition Trust. Globally, a very positive indicator is the United Nations Convention on Biodiversity. This endeavour seeks a multinational consensus to provide massive funding for the preservation of ecosystems in developing nations and aims to place at least a third of the planet under protective conservation.

PL: *I can't help but wonder about the significance of the name Adam in 'Crossroads', and about the biblical and indigenous themes in* Cries from the Ark. *Could you tell us about the role of religion, mythology, and history in your work?*

DM: A character in Brian Moore's novel, *The Statement*, expresses the thought, "History is an echo." History, religion, and myth all echo in my work. In the 'fallen' world of 'Crossroads', paradise still echoes.

PL: *How does research factor into your writing, both for poetry and prose?*

DM: Typically, I write from what I know, what has engaged me. After the work has been framed, I often will conduct research in order to correct or elaborate.

PL: *Have you fallen down any interesting rabbit holes of research?*

DM: Recently, I wrote a couple of poems about carnivorous plants — and then followed up with some fact-checking, and got 'ensnared' by Charles Darwin's *Insectivorous Plants*.

PL: *Are there any Canadian poets or writers you read again and again?*

DM: A partial list of short fiction writers includes Morley Callaghan, Zsuzsi Gartner, Jack Hodgins, Alistair MacLeod, Alice Munro, and Ayelet Tsabari. A partial list of poets is Margaret Avison, Earle Birney, Leonard Cohen, Lorna Crozier, Julia McCarthy, Don McKay, and Jan Zwicky. And for writers in both forms, my partial list is Margaret Atwood, Michael Crummey, and Matt Rader.

PL: *What's the best piece of writing advice you have received?*

DM: Dylan Thomas's 'In my Craft or Sullen Art' has the line, "I labour by singing light." Through many readings, the phrase still resonates how writing requires diligence and inspiration.

PL: *Here at* Pulp Literature, *we have come to know many lawyer-poets such as yourself. Do you have any thoughts on this seemingly curious marriage of identities?*

DM: Poets and lawyers play with words — *homo ludens*. Each takes delight in expression. Also, lawyers, like poets, have a limited readership. Who reads the dexterous fine print in a mortgage or warranty? Mostly other lawyers. Sadly, lawyering pays better than making poetry. To quote out of context Dickens's Joe Gargery from *Great Expectations*, "poetry costs money." Hence, the practice of law can subsidize the practice of poetry.

Non-lawyer writers, aware of the game aspect of the law, can tend toward satire. Jonathan Swift said, "Laws are like cobwebs, which may catch small flies, but let wasps and hornets break through." Poets and/or lawyers should take up brooms and clear away those dusty cobwebs.

PL: *Thank you for making the time to speak with us. Before we go, could you tell us about your current projects?*

DM: I am working on a collection of stories mostly set on Vancouver Island. The opening story is 'The Widow', which appeared in the *Dalhousie Review*.

Selected Bibliography

Books

Cries from the Ark, London, Ontario: Brick Books, 2017.

Poetry and Short Fiction

'The Broken Voice', *you are a flower growing off the side of a cliff*, volume one, ed. Rayanne Haines, Toronto: League of Canadian Poets, 2021.

'Black Bear: Spring Feeding', *Spring Peepers*, ed. Ronda Wicks, Toronto: Beret Days Press, 2021, 18.

'Birthday Letter', *Voicing Suicide*, ed. Daniel G Scott, Victoria, BC: Ekstasis Editions, 2020, 105–106.

'American Bullfrog', *Sweet Water: Poems for the Watersheds*, ed. Yvonne Blomer, Halfmoon Bay, BC: Caitlin Press, 2020, 127.

'Uriah' and 'Miriam', *Poetica Magazine Anna Davidson Rosenberg Award Collection 2017–2018*, Norfolk, Virginia: Poetica Publishing, 2019, 10 and 13.

'Lamb', *As You Were: The Military Review* (US) 11 (Autumn 2019).

'The Skinny on Putting on Skinny Jeans — A 12 Step Program,' *Defenestration Magazine* (US) (January 2, 2019).

'Parrotfish,' *Refugium, Poems for the Pacific*, ed. Yvonne Blomer, Halfmoon Bay, BC: Caitlin Press, 2017, 149.

'Cherry-RIPE', *The Linnet's Wings* (US), (Summer 2016), 28–35.

'The Riddle', *Brittle Star* (UK), Issue 35 (Winter 2014), 66–71.

'Pig-meat', *Stand* (UK) 201, 12:1 (2013), 61–66.

'The Widow', *The Dalhousie Review* 92.1/2 (Spring/Summer 2012), 45–50.

PULP
Literature
Good books for the price of a beer
Allaigna's Song   Overture   JM Landels
PULP Literature
Short stories, poetry, and comics you can't put down
www.pulpliterature.com

GHOST WALKING

Mel Anastasiou

Mel Anastasiou writes ghost stories and mysteries, including the Fairmount Manor Mysteries, the Monument Studios Mysteries, and the Hertfordshire Pub Mysteries, available at pulpliterature. com. Her novel Stella Ryman and the Fairmount Manor Mysteries won a Literary Titan Gold Book Award and was shortlisted for the Stephen Leacock Medal for Humour. 'Ghost Walking' is an excerpt from her forthcoming novel, Pretty Lies, an Orpheus tale in a classic British Columbia setting.

Ghost Walking

Chapter 1

Howe Sound, Summer 1974

The ferryboat rocked along sunlit Howe Sound waters on course for Bowen Island. It carried a full load this afternoon in early July. On the car deck, doors slammed and children raced in and out among the vehicles. Up here on the Sunshine Deck, foot passengers milled about and craned at the shoreline and mountains. Jenny Riley looked back. Her determined departure from university life, via this crowded ferryboat, was entirely different from the way Joey had left the world: in the rain, at night, slipping out of her arms while gasoline pooled through shattered windshield glass into the weeds by the road.

A boy in a windbreaker ran up beside her and leaned too far out over the rail. He opened his fist and let go of a *Sweet Marie* candy wrapper so that the red-and-yellow paper swooped up and then fell into the ferryboat wake. It was a long way down.

Jenny caught his arm. "Don't you want to live to grow up,

litterbug boy? Don't lean so far out."

"You're not the boss of me." He pulled free, stuck his chocolate bar into his mouth like a fat cigar, and tore off down the stairs to the deck below.

Jenny leaned over the rail to watch the waves slap the ferry's side. A light spray from the ferry's bow brushed cold fingers against her cheek. *Joey?*

A man said, "Don't lean so far over."

You're not the boss of me. Jenny narrowed her eyes against the sun. Beside her a young BC Ferries officer rested his arms on the rail, sleeves rolled up above his elbows. His body cut the wind so that the full heat of the sun fell on her shoulders, and she shaded her eyes with her hand. He didn't look much older than she was. How on earth did you get to be a ferry officer so young? She, now twenty-two, had no more idea than a puppy of what she wanted to do with her life. A seagull flapped overhead, a French fry hanging from its beak. It occurred to Jenny that it didn't take much for a seagull to lead a happy existence.

She said, "Are you in charge? Those kids are tearing everywhere. It can't be safe."

"You know kids, they don't listen. And I tell you what, it's always been the same. In the old days, fellows used to jump off the dock pilings while the boat pulled away. The Union Steamships. Party ships full of drunks. Leaping fools."

"Reckless. Why?"

"Who knows? The reckless ones won't tell you. And half the world is reckless."

"What about the other half?"

"The other half tries to keep the reckless ones safe. I'm going to find those kids and burn their ears for them."

"The other half thanks you." Jenny looked more closely at the ferry officer. How had she thought this was a young man? He was in his sixties, with grizzled salt-and-pepper hair. Next to her arm on the railing, the back of his hand bulged with blue veins. He followed her gaze, let go of the rail, and moved away down the same steps the kid had. The truth was that, since the accident, she'd stopped believing her eyes. And the reason for that was the frequency with which she saw Joey on the street, walking briskly in jean cut-offs, shaggy blond head nodding; Joey framed in a bus window or tipping back a beer outside a liquor store.

But not here. Jenny scanned the bucket seats that ran along the centre of the Sunshine Deck, where a few determined readers snapped and folded their newspapers against the wind. A woman with a baby tapped her cigarette into the tin ashtray on the seat beside her, pulled a blanket across her chest, and set her baby to nurse. A young woman with green ribbons in her hair wove among the seats. She was about Jenny's age, and her step was so dancelike that Jenny had to wonder whether she was on something. The other Sunshine Deck passengers ignored her.

A half dozen more rowdy little boys in yellow T-shirts cackled and shoved each other against the railing nearest the ferryboat's bow. One of them crashed into Jenny and hit the railing hard. "Stop him, will you?" a young Chinese man said, apparently to the Sunshine Deck at large.

The kid ran off. He seemed to know a lot of swear words but not the word *sorry*.

"Sorry," the Chinese guy mumbled, and moved away.

Somebody nearby called out, "Not as sorry as you're going

to be for the next two weeks with those kids." A blond fellow in his early twenties lay, with one arm across his eyes, on a box stencilled *Life Jackets*. He looked exactly like Joey.

Another camper cut in front of her, followed by the Chinese guy, whose shirt had come untucked at the back.

He said, "Sorry about that."

"That's two *sorries* from you today," she said.

"God, and you're so pretty. Sorry." He tore away again, down the steps and out of sight.

She moved towards the fellow feigning sleep on the life-jacket box, the one who looked like Joey. Or appeared to look like Joey. He said, "It's no wonder people send their kids away."

He didn't sound like Joey, and that was a relief. Still, she had to reckon with the way he sprawled like a sleeping dog, and the thick blond bangs that fell across his face. His eyes were closed, as if he were talking in his sleep.

He said, "Parents ship their children off to school or camp, get them the hell out of the house. I feel their pain. My name's Adrian. What's yours?"

"Jenny."

He nodded. "And parents send their grown daughters and sons away because they do drugs or fall in love with the wrong person. That what happened to you?"

"I sent myself, thanks very much."

"So no passion in it for you on this epic, twenty-minute journey from the mainland? Poor Jenny." Adrian folded his arms behind his head the way Joey used to do, and stretched out his legs over the edge of the crate. Over by the rail, the Chinese guy hung onto two small boys by the backs of their T-shirts.

Adrian added, "Well, it might be worse, you know. What if

you were a camp counsellor like him and had to babysit those damned kids? The tiny, mindless pups."

"You couldn't pay me enough to do a job like that."

"The punchline is that it barely pays anything at all." Adrian sat up on the crate. "Why doesn't Malcolm let that damn kid jump to his death? I'm going to get no sleep with the idiotic way he's doing his job. He's right, though, you're a looker. I like you long-haired women."

Jenny said, "Thanks, but my sister says the pretty girls are awful."

"Yeah, like purple Smarties. And summer jobs at summer camps that look easy until you meet the campers. I could be making the same money working at Peter's on Broadway, where there are smoke breaks and I can suck at the milkshake teat." Adrian stretched and moved away from her. On the back of his T-shirt she read in bold print the word *Counsellor*.

She shook her head. So much like Joey. And nothing like him at all. Possibly she was safe from hallucinations on the ferryboat. In which case, maybe she should stay here forever, sailing back and forth, like the ferryman Charon across the River Styx, but without his boatload of ghosts. And no fare to pay if you never disembarked. Bonus.

Snug Cove's cluster of island homes and shops grew bigger as the ferry pushed through the waves towards Bowen. Around her, passengers stubbed out cigarettes and drifted towards the stairs. The odd young woman in her flowered dress and green hair ribbons sat down next to an older man. He glanced at his watch and closed his newspaper. She leaned towards him as if to speak, but the man stood up, shoved his paper into his armpit, and walked away without a backward glance. Jenny would have liked to ask him why he was so unkind to a young woman with obvious problems. But perhaps he had ridden the ferry with her before and learned his lesson. Or maybe he was a jerk.

The ferry bumped against a piling and skewed sideways as it found a fit into its slip. Seagulls cried from the zinc-capped pilings. On the dock, a half dozen cars rumbled up to the rails and stopped, ready to pick up passengers.

A battered green Galaxie 500 took up more than its share of the dock. Jenny made out the familiar figure of her father's cousin Frances Riley climbing out of the driver's door. She wore a black T-shirt and shorts, and her long grey hair was tied back with a leather thong. She had the determined Riley chin. Jenny took one look at it and made her second grand decision in as many months. She would stay on the boat and ride back to the mainland for free. She'd phone Frances from a pay phone, apologize for her change of mind, and she'd deal with her mental crisis on her own. *Thank you, sorry, and goodbye.*

The girl in the flowered dress drifted up beside her at the deck rail, her skirt and hair ribbons flapping in the wind. She stood a little too close.

"Here's a story that will interest you," the young woman said. "Once there was a young woman who was so much in love with her boyfriend that she wanted nothing but him."

One thing months of counselling had done for Jenny was equip her to recognize a one-size-fits-all statement when she heard it. She said, "Are you talking about you or me?"

"Both of us, sister. I'm Moira." Moira moved even closer. "You?"

By now Jenny had a pretty good idea why everybody on this ship looked right through Moira. But she didn't want to be a jerk. "Jenny Riley."

Moira nodded as if she had guessed it already. "My fellow is called Philip, and he's a true heart, a true love, to stick by truly through thick and thin. We're together forever."

Together forever. That's what Joey had said.

Moira looked closely at her. "Oh, cats. I'm sorry. But he'll take you back, won't he?"

Jenny shook her head.

Moira brightened. "Forget your cares. Let's stay on the boat, and we can ride back and forth all day together."

Jenny looked down at Adrian on the ferry deck, lazing against the bow while the ramp descended, looking up at her and smiling. She smiled back.

Moira put her arm across Jenny's shoulder. "Let's become stowaways together. What do you say?"

Jenny freed herself gently and swung her backpack onto her shoulder. "Got to go. My cousin's waiting on the dock."

If Moira protested, Jenny didn't hear her. She clanged down the two stairways to the car deck and joined the swell of foot passengers massed at the bow of the boat, behind the safety chain that two ferry workers held across the low open front. The old ferry officer she'd spoken to earlier waved off the foot passengers ahead of the cars. In front of her, the campers scuttled after Malcolm and Adrian.

Jenny legged it up the ramp towards the dock, where her cousin Frances took her backpack and hefted it into the back seat of the Galaxie. "Welcome. Like old times, isn't it? Except for the accident, sadly. I want to help you with that, but let me remind you — I'm nobody's mother."

"I remember."

"Stupendous. Climb in, and don't mess up the jumble."

Jenny asked, "Can I jumble up the mess?"

"Damn. I forgot you have an oblique mind." Frances slid into the driver's seat.

"Not really. I was trying to be funny." Jenny climbed in beside her and hauled on the Galaxie's door. It took both hands to pull it shut. "Of course, it's good of you to have me, and I'm happy to be here."

"So you're oblique, polite, and as restfully insincere as you were as a child. What a combination."

Jenny smiled. "I bet you'd rather it was Rachel coming to stay."

"Is it true your sister talks only in poetry now?"

"Rachel recites lines from *Desiderata*, appropriate to all occasions."

"So you're both poisoned chalices? I'd rather have you, then." Frances put the Galaxie into drive and then stomped on the brake as a pickup truck with *Camp Vehicle* painted on the driver's door cut them off and growled past with a shifting mountain of duffels and sleeping bags tied in its bed. The boy campers and their two counsellors followed the pickup on foot, in an uncertain line towards the old general store and the shops and restaurants that lined the road. For such a small island, Jenny thought, there was a lot of traffic. She looked back at the ferry.

Moira in her summer dress, green ribbons in her hair, stood in the middle of the ferry deck. Cars loaded to each side of her while she gazed towards shore. Jenny raised a hand in farewell.

Frances hunched over the Galaxie's steering wheel. "You're difficult, but you've always been difficult under your manners. And that's fine by me. I had a difficult father, and I've been difficult myself in my time. More than you, I bet."

"Maybe everybody is difficult."

"Maybe everybody interesting is difficult. Listen, I think it's best to ask up front. I understand that you're grieving, but are you suicidal?"

Jenny looked Frances in the eye. "Is there a third selection on the menu?"

"Well, there's crazy."

Jenny turned around in her seat and peered out the Galaxie's rear window. The ferry pulled away from the dock. At the rear of the car deck, closest to the dock, Moira sat dangling her feet from the flat stern of the ferry. She lowered herself over the side and slipped lightly from the boat deck into the ferry's wash.

She should have gone under, but she didn't.

Instead, and against all the world's logic, Moira in her flowered dress walked across the surface of the water, heading out towards the Sound. The waves flashed sunlight upwards, like flames under her feet.

Jenny pressed her face against the seat back.

"Hang on." Frances thudded the Galaxie into drive.

Jenny hung on. When she looked again, the Galaxie was turning the corner at the top of the hill and the Cove was out of sight.

CHAPTER 2

Jenny woke with, as her sister Rachel would say, a good strong dose of the 'peace there may be in silence'. In fact, there was so much peace in the guest bedroom that Jenny felt driven to break it by dumping her backpack contents across the unmade guest bed. Rachel's gifts scattered across the sheets, clear messages of sisterly concern in strawberry Lip Smacker, Avon Sweet Honesty, and a copy — handwritten in multi-pen — of *Desiderata*. Rachel, who kept sixteen stuffed penguins lined up at the head of her bed, all facing east, was worried about her.

Jenny walked to the window, breathed on the glass, and wrote with the tip of her finger, *Wherever you go, there you are.* And in fact here also was her younger sister, along with the pro bono grief therapist from university. She pictured him now, telling her to write her wishes on his office window in the fog of her breath with her finger. He said he wouldn't look because he was meant to be a blind oracle, but she was sure he was only bored with his own process, eyes shut, lounging on that grubby acid-green sofa. She imagined him saying again, "Look past the writing and tell me, what do you see?"

Jenny looked past her glass writing to Frances's hemlock-shadowed driveway. She saw foxgloves and Shasta daisies, but she didn't see Moira. Which was not the worst start to the morning, until the bushes next to the cabin shivered as if something large had exhaled on them. Branches parted, and a small boy with a stick appeared. Jenny leaned her forehead against the window. The kid looked real, but then so had Moira until she'd walked on water.

The boy's attention appeared to be completely focused on the stick in his hand. He swung it at a stand of foxgloves, narrowly missing the Galaxie's tail light. Purple flowers scattered across the trunk of the car. He followed up with a couple of clanking swipes at a drainpipe at the corner of the house and then raised the stick over his shoulder and slashed his way along some sword ferns. As he turned to murder another foxglove, Jenny caught sight of the large black word stamped across his yellow T-shirt: *Camper*.

So this brat, now kicking at a heap of kindling stored beneath the back steps, was as real as Jenny was. She'd probably seen him on the ferry yesterday, in the dubious care of those two counsellors.

A rap at the door made her jump.

"I'm just off the phone with your sister Rachel," Frances said through the door. "She told me how you sat all night in the garage inside the wrecked car."

"I think I was looking for him in the last place I saw him," Jenny said. "And that was in the car where he died. To say goodbye, you know."

"I'll bet that seemed reasonable until you said it out loud. I've been reading up, and I found some ideas on how to help you. Come on out to the porch. Coffee's ready when you are."

Jenny walked past the galley kitchen to the bright living room. She slid open the living room's plate-glass door and stepped onto the porch. The view was nonpareil, across the empty blue Sound to the green hills of Gambier Island.

Frances crossed the deck and stood beside her, looking out to sea. She said, "I guess you're here because of the way my father died."

"A bit, but I've always liked visiting you," Jenny said. "Can I ask, how long did it take you to mourn him?"

"Still proceeding."

"But it did get easier as time went on?"

"Work helps." Frances taught archaeology at university.

Jenny said, "I dropped my courses."

"Butterfingers. But don't you think it will be different for you anyway? In the case of the death of a person your own age, you'll feel not only shock but anger at the unfairness of the loss."

"My grief counsellor would agree with you."

Frances cleared her throat. A moment before, her hands had been empty, but now she was holding a book, her thumb marking a page partway through. "I've been reading up on alternative therapies for grief. I found one called the Primal Scream. Do you think you might try that?"

Jenny said, "I think I won't, thank you. I'd actually like to be quiet. To recover on a peaceful island away from constant reminders, you know the kind of thing."

"Apparently Primal Scream is a successful therapy."

"Screaming is really not necessary."

"And yet I'd argue that you do scream, only silently. The book says to let it out."

"Where's that coffee? Can I pour you some?" Jenny left her for the kitchen. "I'm going to cook something for us."

"Rachel says you don't eat."

"I eat. Do I look like I don't eat? I'll eat breakfast."

"Help yourself. Eat anything you like."

Help herself, heal herself. Here went nothing. Jenny swung open the door of the curvaceous, elderly fridge. Inside she saw only three opened bottles of Coffee-mate, a box of cheese, celery, and eggs.

"Why eggs?" Jenny asked. "Everything else in here starts with C."

"I'm not much for cooking. But I'm a good researcher." Frances leaned her elbows on the kitchen counter. "Primal Screaming is supposed to work if you're too repressed and quiet—are you too quiet?"

"Can someone be too quiet?"

On the counter, a short stack of blue plates and a mug full of cutlery stood beside a saucer of butter and a yellow bowl. Jenny broke four eggs into the bowl and stirred them with a fork until they foamed up pale yellow. She turned the stove up high, opened a drawer, and slung a frying pan onto the burner.

Frances said, "What if we consider your future?"

"I see eggs in my future, and yours too." She cut a lump of butter into the hot pan and poured in the eggs.

"I understand why you sound angry," Frances said, "Your boyfriend died in a crash. You must be furious with him, breaking up with you that way."

"I see what you're trying to do, Frances. And maybe I came here partly because you talk like this. But here's something to think about: a counsellor recently told me that I should cook for myself and others as a productive therapy." She rolled the sizzling eggs to the edge of the pan.

"How does cooking eggs resolve a relationship when the fellow isn't alive anymore?"

"You get on with everyday life after somebody important to you dies, and apparently it involves recovery at its most basic human level. Getting food."

"That counsellor sounds like a wet rag. What if you turn your attention away from the past, as if you'd split up with your boyfriend the regular way? There's a Roman dig in England this summer, and it's mine if I want it. Come with me."

Jenny asked, "I've always wondered whether it's kind to dig up ancient dead people."

"Yes, of course it is." Frances rolled her eyes. "But this is a mosaic dig. No dead bodies. The mosaic floor is buried in a hypocaust. And for once in my semi-illustrious career, I've beaten old man Chalmers to it. I'm going to dig up the mosaic and reassemble it for display at the British Museum."

Jenny folded the omelette in half, tipped it, golden and glazed with butter, onto a blue plate, and handed it to Frances.

Jenny said, "See, I feel better for that."

Frances took a bite and grinned at her. "Do you?"

Jenny almost smiled. "No." *Yes.* But the smell of the eggs made her want to throw up.

Frances pointed her fork at Jenny. "You're stubborn in the manner of the ancient Stoics, I think, except if you were really a Stoic, you'd be happy about it. Look, come along to the dig in England and start forgetting your Joey a little bit. Get your hands dirty. Work cures everything."

Jenny said, "Bowen Island is as far as I want to go."

"It would be a good way to get you over your breakup."

"That's what they told Juliet," Jenny said. "And also Ophelia. It didn't work."

"What a trio—you, Juliet, and Ophelia. If there's one thing Shakespeare teaches us, it's that nothing in the world can come between a stubborn young woman and her no-good first love. You think you'll be together forever."

Together forever. Jenny left the kitchen and strode through the living room, through the glass door onto the porch. She held tight to the porch rail as if she were standing at the bow of a ship on high seas. She took a long breath and ground out a scream so loud and rough—almost male in tone—that it reminded her of raucous nights with Joey's friends.

She stopped screaming because the memory frightened her, or else she stopped because her throat hurt. From behind her she heard the door to the porch slide shut. Still forking egg from her plate, Frances stood beside her at the porch rail. "Did that help?"

"No." Jenny wrapped her arms around her stomach.

Frances swallowed her mouthful of egg. "It was not a bad scream. You used your diaphragm, though. You're supposed to scream with your head voice."

Frances let loose a scream that ran a nail through Jenny's skull.

"Oh, God," Jenny said. "Frances, what do you want from me?"

"Here, eat the rest of these eggs." Frances offered Jenny her plate.

"Unlikely."

Frances tipped the eggs over the porch rail and shoved the blue plate at her. "Break this."

"Even more unlikely." Jenny balanced the plate on the rail. If she'd had to, she would have jumped off the porch to get away from Frances, but all she had to do was turn and walk away from her into the house.

So she did. She walked straight into the sliding glass door. It banged and then cracked. She jumped back out of the way of the crashing knives of glass. Shards rained from the door frame onto the porch and the living room floor.

"You couldn't just break the dish?" Frances asked.

Jenny left Frances standing barefoot on the porch, while she, in her running shoes, leapt over the broken glass. She walked through the living room and out the back door. The spray of broken blossoms the child had made with his stick still lay across the hood of the Galaxie. She swept them away with her hand and saw that the key was in the ignition.

Without pausing to think, she climbed inside. She set her right hand on the steering wheel and rested her left on the open window ledge, like some boy cruising Monterey. She hadn't driven since the crash, but she felt at ease against the Naugahyde seats. Sitting here at the wheel, she wasn't a tragic victim; she was simply a houseguest stealing her hostess's Ford Galaxie 500. Jenny turned the key and rolled the Galaxie down the long forest drive.

CHAPTER 3

The Galaxie's dashboard clock showed that it was only ten o'clock, and Jenny was interested to see how quickly a visit could go wrong. She topped the hill above the Cove and turned down it with a rattle of gravel under the Galaxie's chassis. The ferry was nowhere in sight, and there was hardly any line-up. Jenny pulled into the parking lot at the Bowen Island General Store. She felt the Galaxie scrape against a concrete block and climbed out of the car to examine the damage. The narrow scratch along the green fender was nearly invisible. She laid her palms on the Galaxie's hood and felt its warmth against her cold hands. *Help yourself, heal yourself.*

Here goes nothing again. She pushed through the door of the general store and discovered that for the first time in months she knew what she wanted. She took a cart with such vigour that she almost rammed a woman wiping down the shelves of canned foods. Jenny picked up a tin of Beefaroni. With its soft noodles and nubs of brown beef, this was the exact product that had steered her sister Rachel to the vegetarian life. Joey had loved it, though, and ate it cold from the can when he was a teenager and would climb from his window into hers in the middle of the night.

Moving briskly, like a smart shopper on TV, Jenny took a box of Freakies cereal off the shelf and tossed it into her cart. She scanned the shelves for sugar, but a smear of red on the shelf where a cereal box had stood caught her attention. She touched the sticky blotch and stared down at the blood on her fingertip.

Imaginary blood or real? She wiped her finger clean on the edge of the shelf.

A voice spoke from behind her. "Bring out your self-exiled maidens."

Blond Adrian, who so reminded her of Joey, leaned back against the pop shelf as if planning a long stay here in the centre aisle of the Bowen Island General Store. He appeared so relaxed, in fact, that a fan of blond hair stood up, uncombed, at the back of his head.

"Hey." She knew why she liked him, and therefore it would be best to walk away from him, to leave him alone in the aisle leaning up against the cardboard six-packs of Crush and Coke. Instead she shoved her shopping cart into the centre of the aisle and looked him dead in the eye. "Adrian. Answer a question for me. Can you see blood on the shelf here?"

"Blood?"

She nodded and stood aside for the cleaning woman, who bumped her grey mop around the cart, up against her shoes and Adrian's, then past them down the aisle.

Adrian said, "I don't see any blood. Are you a vampire? And even if you are, wouldn't you rather drink Mountain Dew?"

"Funny. But look, it's right here." She moved a box of Corn Chex to one side. There was no blood on the shelf after all. "Of course not. The cleaner's been by."

The cleaning woman hurried back towards Jenny. "Is this yours?" She held up a green hair ribbon.

Jenny shook her head. She set both hands on her cart to stop them shaking.

The woman tossed the ribbon into her trash bag.

At the far end of the aisle, the other camp counsellor from the day before, the one called Malcolm, gesticulated at a group of yappy boys in yellow shirts. One of them had a stick tucked in his shorts belt loop like a sword.

Malcolm called, "Adrian, it's your turn to keep them out of the candy aisle."

"I refuse to remove any living creature from its natural environment," Adrian said.

Jenny hardly heard them, for now there appeared to be blood on the floor at her feet. She looked up as Malcolm approached.

"The manager's going to kick the kids out, but it's not safe for them in the parking lot. Will you go watch them? I'm getting marshmallows for campfire later. Hello again," Malcolm said to Jenny, stepping around her shopping cart. His left sandal almost touched the small pool of red on the linoleum between them.

Malcolm took a step backwards. "Is that blood?"

"You see it too?" She felt a sharp sting and looked at her hand. A drop of red trailed off the end of her ring finger and fell to the floor.

"What have you done to yourself? I've got my St John's certificate." Malcolm took her hand in his and turned it so that the pale skin inside her wrist lay upwards. Along the inside of her arm ran a short, straight red line, as if someone had drawn it there with a ruler and the sharp tip of a compass. It was a very fine and narrow cut to have produced such a pool of blood. It seemed to be closing now.

"It doesn't look like you'll need stitches." Malcolm released her. "How'd you cut yourself?"

"I don't know." She hardly noticed she was lying sometimes, which was a knee-jerk product of life with Joey. But she corrected herself. "Well, I walked through a window."

Malcolm's look of anxiety, and Adrian's of amused disbelief, made her wish she'd stuck with the lie. And suddenly she'd had enough of both of them. She raised the hand of her injured arm in farewell and walked away from them and from her half-filled grocery cart in the middle of the aisle. She jogged out of the store empty-handed — red-handed — and across the parking lot, where two of the little boys had climbed up on the Galaxie's front bumper and were bouncing up and down. It wasn't worth the trouble to scold them, or even to haul open the big heavy car door and get back inside it. The white crown of the ferryboat's upper deck showed beyond the trees on the point. She broke into a run, heading downhill. Her runners made no sound on the blacktop as she trotted past the little shops and cafés lining the road to the ferry dock. An old man called out to her from the steps of the Bow-Mart Café, but she couldn't make out his words.

She curled her fingers around her sticky right palm and looked out at the incoming ferryboat. It approached swiftly, shining white in the sun. A yawl with red sails slipped along behind it. Even at this distance, the ferry's grinding engines sounded clearly. Up top, along the Sunshine Deck rail, the passengers in bright summer T-shirts hung like a row of flapping flags. She didn't see Moira, praise all powers, and not a single person was walking on the water. Even more reassuringly, the blood she'd seen on the floor at the general store was real blood, from her own arm, cut without her noticing when she'd smashed Frances's sliding porch door.

So, this morning, this was the lesson she had to master: logic was everything, even when dealing with grief and post-trauma hallucinations. All she had to do was ask herself a question: *Is the object or person I am seeing or hearing connected in any way with impossible events?* If the answer was yes, then what she saw was not real. It was a nice binary solution to seeing ghosts. She breathed in relief, a long slow intake of reassurance. When she breathed out, the sky dimmed. But, she reasoned with her newfound logic, her exhaled breath had not actually caused the change in weather. It had to be that rain was threatening, as rain certainly will do on the Northwest Coast.

But this was not a typical grey BC sky descending over the Cove. On the contrary, it darkened from cerulean to indigo blue, against which stars shone in their constellations. All this in the middle of a sunlit summer morning. Jenny ran out to the end of the wharf closest to the ferry slip. And there stood Moira at the rail amongst a group of noisy passengers in formal dress. At the bow end, lit by deck lights, a young ship's officer stood alone, tall and handsome in his white shirt and black trousers.

No one should see night in day. Or hear unexplained music, brassy and slow. Two men in jackets and slacks leaped, crowing, from the dock pilings into the sea, arms wide and eyes screwed up, to the shouts and applause of onlookers in party dress on the Sunshine Deck.

Then starlight passed away, and with it the young men in the water and Moira at the rail. The sunny morning returned, and the boat deck was crowded with passengers in shorts and T-shirts, standing ready to disembark.

If it's impossible, then it's not true. She closed her eyes and opened them. It was still daylight. There was nothing wrong with dreaming, if you knew you were dreaming. You were only insane if you believed the pictures in your head.

So she was sane — as long as she discounted the perfect clarity of her vision and the way the shadows had disappeared when night blotted out the daytime sky.

On board the ferryboat, engines sounded. The big steel ramp dropped against the dock. Jenny trailed the queue of cars up the hill to the store parking lot and climbed into the Galaxie. The little boys in their yellow camp shirts had cleared the lot, and when she turned the Galaxie onto the road, she saw ahead of her the long string of campers in their yellow T-shirts, trudging up the hill from Snug Cove. She drove along the line, and both counsellors waved. After a moment, she returned the gesture, but too late. She'd already rounded the top of the hill. It didn't matter.

Yes it did. She caught her error the second after she made it. Reality mattered terribly.

The casting call is murder

COMING SOON FROM

PULP LITERATURE PRESS

JUST ANOTHER DATE NIGHT ON THE HIGHWAY OUT OF TOWN

Zandra Renwick

Zandra Renwick's *short stories have been translated, podcasted, performed on stage, and developed for television. When not propping up the walls of her crumbling stone home in the heart of Canada's capital city, she curates prenested vintage goods on the hip SoCo strip near downtown Austin, Texas. Find more about her writing at zandrarenwick.com.*

Just Another Date Night on the Highway Out of Town

This girl Spider brought along on what he and I have been calling our weekly double-date hell night is so annoying because she's saying stuff like, *Of course I love pizza as much as everybody else, but is it gluten-free?* So I'm looking at Spider sitting across from me in this raggy sliced-up Naugahyde booth in the back of what everybody on campus knows is the rankest late-night highway pizza dive in creation and I'm thinking, Spider, dude, it's a fact we're still friends despite you cheating on me, like, two years ago and me dumping your squeaky ass, but I know what you've got down those baggy pants of yours is nothing even close to gluten-free. Then I think maybe it's all moot because his sad gluteny manbits never do actually pass her lips and then I start thinking, Joke's on you, Spider; I may not be half as pretty as this girl but at least I always prided myself on giving decent reciprocal tit for what was, to be fair, your enthusiastic and sometimes not uncreative tat.

I thank again the god I never believed in that I'm dating Shelly now, but it's astounding I even have to point out the obvious fact for like the fifth time that, gluten-free or not, this effing pizza in front of us has a fake black-polished fingernail sticking straight up out of the centre, a pointy Halloween talon rising from soupy yellow cheese like a mini black obelisk from a mozzarella moor.

Turning the scratched plastic pitcher upside down to get the last dregs of un-gluten-free beer into my glass, I'm thinking, Okay, sure, it's the middle of the week and the middle of the night and we're in the middle of nowhere, but it's still telling that we're the only customers in this joint. I picture some idiot back there in the kitchen slinging dough into big metal ovens, not caring if her tacky vampire press-ons aren't staying pressed. Figuring I'm the only one at the table with the balls or maybe the brains to go complain to management, I knock back my beer and kiss my girlfriend Shelly and stand. Shelly doesn't seem to mind Spider's idiot date, and they're chattering away about manicures and gluten-free crusts, both shining examples of the kind of normal girl I will forever fail to be. I pretend not to be a little jealous as I heft our gross pizza and stomp over to the counter to complain about its surprise extra topping and try to weasel a free second pitcher on the house while they sling us up a new pie.

The guy behind the counter looks culled from a casting call for sleazy roadside diner characters, like some low-budget movie director needed a night fry cook for the kind of horror film my grandma watched at the drive-in over my granddaddy's shoulder from the backseat—you know, like he'd gut you with a fillet knife or grind you up for burgers: stubble, bloodshot eyes, dirty white apron with stains the shapes of tiny continents or exposed internal organs straight out of used dollar-bin textbooks.

Excuse me, I tell him, *but there's a fake fingernail in the cheese in the middle of our pizza. Some kind of claw-looking thingy.*

He turns from the muted television flickering behind the bar and blinks once, slow and rusty, like it's the first time he's blinked in so long he's forgotten how. He takes me in — my untucked plaid flannel and my oversized combats and my black eyeliner and my holey black jeans and my cropped ironic headbanger mullet — and I feel judged AF.

I plop the pizza on the counter between us. Grease spills over the rim of the cooling metal plate. *There is a fingerfuckingnail,* I tell him, *embedded in the fucking cheese of our fuckeroni pizza.*

Embedded, he echoes.

Everyone says locals resent us college kids from up the road, and I wonder if he's making a comment on my vocabulary. Like he's saying that if I were a tea drinker, I'd lift my pinkie. Like, maybe he's saying I'm super fancy for using precise language, for using a word like *embedded.* But then without looking down at the pizza he says, *It probably didn't get enough time in the incubator.*

The eerie monotone way he says it doesn't sound like he's making fun. And *incubator* is fancier than any term I would've come up with for a pizza oven. It's having-the-queen-for-tea and pinkie-lifting kind of fancy. Seriously, his expression is deadpan, no funny business at all.

I'm still pondering an appropriate reply when he starts filling me a new pitcher brimming with beer. I hear Shelly's cute little shiny laugh and turn to see her leaning across the gouged table to touch Spider's date's left earring. Shelly's a flirt and a sweetheart and not at all like lying cheatmonger Spider, but that same stupid jealousy stabs deep in my gut to see how easy it is for her, for all of them. It's like everyone got some class in confidence that I never found in the syllabus. Like they all graduated Social Ease 101, working on their BAs in b-s.

When I turn back the barman is gone, along with the pizza. The beer is there, though, frothy and golden, fresh from the tap — the only reason anyone comes to this place at all.

Second pitcher down and things are brighter than before. Glowier. Fuzzier and nicer. I don't drink often, but I love the way beer softens the edges of my social anxiety. Much more fun than my usual coping mechanism: avoiding other people altogether. Spider's telling stories about him and me growing up next door to each other in the next state over, describing the glittery banana seat on my bike when we were kids, the tassels I used to tape to my handlebars, and the playing cards we used to stick in his spokes. Shelly is warm and soft, laughing at Spider's stupid jokes, snuggled against my side. Even Spider's date seems less annoying than she did an hour ago — not cool, exactly, but not terrible. The second pizza is delivered to our table without a word, plunked down by a stocky blonde with short bitten nails who doesn't look imaginative enough in her fashion choices to wear the offending item contaminating our last order. There's something about her familiar flat bloodshot gaze that makes me think she must be related to the barman. She blinks once at me before shuffling away, a long slow rusted blink like her eyelids are on unoiled hinges and can barely function.

By now we're all a little sloshed — except Spider's date, who won't drink our gluten-riddled beer and is fiddling with her phone the way certain types of skinny girls do when everyone else is eating. The rest of us each grab hot cheesy slices to stuff in our pie-holes. Spider has wolfed down half his slice already without chewing when Shelly's expression turns weird and she spits out her mouthful onto the scarred tabletop. She gags, reaching into her mouth, scooping out a congealed-cheese mass of dough and red sauce studded with unidentifiable gooey flecks and small gristle-jointed bones that remind me of the baby pig knuckles the highway truck stop near my hometown keeps in a big jar next to the register.

I start spitting chunks of my pizza into the fistful of napkins I've yanked from the chrome dispenser in the middle of the table. Spider puts what's left of his slice back on the greasy metal plate. Shelly jumps up and runs to the bathroom, and Spider's date follows her. I'm too mesmerized by the twitching chunks flopping around on the surface of our pizza to feel more than a brief pang of jealousy at the notion someone else is taking care of my girlfriend in her moment of distress.

Spider? I say, and he says, *Yeah?* And I say, *That wasn't a fake press-on costume nail in our pizza before, was it.* (I say it like that: not really asking.) And, looking a little green, he answers, *No.*

I'm going to assume it's because of the beer that I decide to lean close enough over the pizza to watch the objects inching through the cheese. You'd think it would be grosser if I recognized what the moving things were, exactly. Like, if they were grubs or maggots or, I don't know, severed human pinkies or embryonic piglets or hatching insects crawling from a clutch of chitinous shells or something. But it's worse not knowing what the hell those things are, squirming and writhing around in their amniotic cheesy sea. Still beer-fuzzed, I reach one finger, tipped in my own chipped midnight-blue nail polish, toward the undulating mass, and gently—baby-hamster gentle! dandelion-fluff gentle!—push back the top layer of clumping yellow cheese.

There's a bubble in the crust underneath, thick and gooey as if not cooked all the way through, or maybe saturated with the thin yellow grease staining the crust more orange than yellow around the edges of the round metal pizza plate. The dough bubble trembles, then parts in the centre. The part widens slowly, blinking wider, wider as if moving on reluctant hinges, until I'm staring straight into a big bloodshot eyeball just like the cook's, like the server's, and it's staring straight back at me.

Spider and I scramble over each other getting out of the booth. My car keys on their chain swinging from my pocket catch on the pitted red vinyl, leaving a deep bloody gouge as I flail away from the table. Spider clutches at my hand, and I grasp his in a mutual panicky clamp as we rush together toward the front door and run straight into the solid, stained-muscleshirted chest of the steely gazed barman.

Not letting go of each other, Spider and I scoot-shuffle backward in the direction of the bathroom where our girls are — which is of course what I meant to do all along. Shelly's the love of my life so far! I'd never leave her to the mercy of a bunch of crazy pizza mofos. As if.

Before we reach the bathroom, the door bangs open and the girls spill out. Past them, the bathroom's grimy industrial wall tiles pulse a sick fluorescent white, limning our blonde server in a halo glow. In both hands she holds a meat cleaver, the sort you might see in one of those drive-in horror flicks my grandmother would've loved. Oh puh-lease, I want to say out loud. I want to roll my eyes, want to make it all seem like a laugh, a prank, like we're getting punked for some low-grade indie webisode. But then Shelly is at my side and she's trembling, and she's crying, and all I want to do is smash in some weirdo pizza-people pie-hole.

The sturdy blonde with the cleaver steps from the bathroom. The barman shambles forward, slack-jawed, looking ready to stab and hack. I plant my feet, force myself to stand straight, take a deep breath and shout, *Wait!*

For a split instant I feel like a rock star. Everyone freezes. Shelly and Spider and Spider's date are shining our-saviour beams at me with their hopeful expressions. The pizza weirdos are watching me too, all bloodshot but calm. Even the googly pizza eyeball——the dough bubble now bloated, stretched to a ridiculous size drooping over the metal plate rim——blinks wide to watch me with what seems like genuinely polite solemnity.

I clear my throat and say, loud and crisp like they try to teach you in public speaking class, *Okay okay okay . . . clearly there's something going on here we don't understand, and we apologize for the intrusion, but now we'll just excuse ourselves and be on our way, and no one needs to get——*

EAT ME, booms the eyeball on the table.

Well, it doesn't boom from the actual eyeball as much as it sort of emanates from the air around the table where the pizza-eye sits, rolling and jiggling. You'd think it would come across as rude——like, if I tell someone to eat me I'm not trying for politeness, you know?——but it doesn't. It doesn't sound angry or threatening or particularly scary at all. What it sounds is desperate. Like it's begging. Begging to be eaten. A pizza, begging to be eaten.

There was this stupid joke we used to tell in frosh opt-in sex positivity circles about how sex was like pizza: when it's good, it's really really good, and when it's bad, it's still pretty good. A few of us might have debated the sex part of that equation, but no one ever denied the universal appeal of pizza. Before now, I would've been hard-pressed to meet a pizza I was unwilling to eat. But that time, I see, has come.

Everyone be cool, I say to Spider and Spider's date and Shelly, but mostly to the pizza and its bloodshot zombie mofo minions. *Everybody be cool, and we'll let ourselves out the back, nice and simple.*

To keep watch on the barman blocking the front entrance, I stumble backward, herding my little crew toward the swinging metal door to the kitchen and the back parking lot and the car and freedom. The pizza eye blinks a doleful blink at me from the Naugahyde booth. The server and barman standing with their kitchen weaponry pointed our direction simultaneously blink along with the pizza, a long dry unhuman motion blasting away any shred of doubt they're functioning as independent agents and not mind-screwed satellites of the jiggling cheesy dough bubble on its round metal plate.

The heavy door swings on surprisingly smooth hinges. I usher the others through behind me without turning and when I'm sure they're all in the kitchen I back in after them, slamming the thick barrel bolt into place. Spinning to hustle everyone out the rear exit, I practically trip over Spider staring slack-jawed at the gaping hole in the kitchen ceiling, the looming treetops and night sky sparkling with frost. Or maybe it's the flying saucer he's staring at, crumpled into the top left side of the enormous commercial oven with its gaping maw spilling a row of what look like unbaked pizza pies onto the filthy concrete floor.

The pizza oven itself is a big round stainless steel dome, and the flat caricature of a UFO disc rides it off kilter like a fat metal beret on a metal giant's bald head. In movies, spaceships are twenty, maybe fifty feet across and aliens look like hairless encephalitic elves with excellent night vision. In reality, spaceships are apparently only about six feet across and aliens look like cheese pizzas.

A weird sound I don't recognize turns out to be Spider crying. *They're all dead,* he's murmuring through his choky sobs. *My lovely delicious crew, all gone, all gone, and home so far away.*

Spider's date moves fast for a skinny girl. She's got Shelly by the hand and is dragging her past the big metal pizza oven/crash-landed flying saucer toward the dark back corner with the glowing red exit sign when a low roundish form scuttles out of the shadows and clamps onto her ankle. I rush to drag the thing off of her, calling to Spider to come help. I'm on the floor, grappling with the curved black talons and segmented pig-knuckle limbs of a small crablike creature the size of a deep-dish personal pizza. It's got these short stumpy stalks with eyeballs at the ends. Three of them. Blinking at me in mournful bloodshot unison.

Spider! I shout, as he steps to the dining room door and draws back the barrel bolt with a loud clank. He opens it wide enough for two more crablike pizza creatures to clickity-clack in on pointy black nails. They're carrying our pizza between them like it's a fallen comrade on a round metal stretcher wedged between their six stumpy eye stalks. In the main restaurant behind them lie two lifeless human-shaped sacks on the floor, their pizza-parlour whites stained with indeterminate continents and organ shapes out of dollar-bin textbooks, with gaping eaten-out holes where their chests should be, deep-dish personal pizza size.

Kicking and tugging, Shelly and I free Spider's date's ankle from the first crab creature and back toward the rear exit. The crab things line up in front of Spider and set the partially eaten pizza on the floor in front of him. The air reverberates again, and again I not so much hear as feel in the bones of my chest the pleading command delivered as mournful edict: *EAT ME.*

Spider sinks to his knees and reaches for the metal pizza plate. I shout his name again. He, all three crabs, and the sorrowful mangled pizza turn their unified bloodshot gazes toward me, differing only in the sizes of their eyeballs, the angles of their stares. But when Spider speaks it's him I hear. His voice with all the layers of our years stripped away: our break-up; our painful stint at dating each other; our mixed-bag moments from kindergarten through high school, sad and happy and painful and amazing. *They need me to make a full crew of four*, he tells me, *but it's okay.* He reaches for the pizza, which closes its weird bubble eye and deflates into his hand when he lifts it to his mouth. He says, *It's already happening, from what I ate before; I'm an incubator, but don't worry, I'll still be me. I'll see more galaxies than humans imagine exist. I'll be the captain, and travel the universe as I eat through my crew, being eaten in return, reborn generation after generation, exploring the cosmos, forever consuming, cycling, recycling, forever hungry, forever sated.*

As he crams the wriggling slice whole into his mouth, I lunge to stop him, but Shelly and Spider's date drag me toward the exit. I'm trying to scream Spider's name but it turns into a hiccupy sob in the centre of my chest, the same spot I see ripping open on Spider where segmented crablike talons push their way through his skin, ribs crumpling inward where there's nothing underneath, a cavity hollowed out, consumed.

Spider's empty body puddles on the floor. The new creature steps daintily from the fleshy mess, flicking the last human goop from its rear talon like you'd shake off damp toilet paper stuck to your shoe.

The door bangs wide. I reel in the sudden cold of outside, my jacket left behind. Fresh air fills my heaving lungs. Shelly yanks my key ring from my pocket, unhooks it from the chain I bought because I wanted to look tough. Her hands shake as she fumbles for my car key. Spider's date is practically carrying me single-handed across the empty parking lot, super strong for a skinny girl. I'm already bargaining with myself about what I saw, what I heard, convincing myself to go back and rescue Spider from whatever inadvertent drug haze or mass hysteria or misunderstood scenario I've just encountered. I'm already concocting a dozen things it could have been or might have been or probably should have been. Anything but what it was.

Spider's date tumbles me into the back seat, crawls in, slams the door. Shelly jams the key in the ignition. Tears are drying in sticky tracks down my aching cheeks. Spider's date clutches me to her chest—surprisingly soft, for a skinny girl—squeezing, rocking us back and forth while my rusty old beater car skids out onto the empty highway back to town. The massive golden flash of igniting outer-space rockets lights up the night, starkly illuminating the tight, frightened features of the other girls in the car. Shelly guns the engine and my crappy balding tires growl at the road. Spider's date and I are tangled arms and hair and breath, watching out the wide rear window together as a dark flat saucer shape blasts upward, making a blazing inferno of what used to be the worst late-night highway pizza dive in creation.

The saucer hangs for a heartbeat, silhouetted against the combined effervescent glare of yellow flames leaping up to meet cool blue jets shooting down. The two flames drift farther apart as the saucer lifts, blue breaking from yellow, both shrinking smaller between the ragged tops of ancient evergreens as we rattle down the country byway. I'm already sad about the rest of my life, about how stars are ruined for me forever, about how shit can come hurtling at you out of nowhere and death isn't always noble or profound, and how no matter what else happens or how long I live, every time I look up into the sky at those countless pinpricks of cold distant flame I'll wonder which one is Spider, eating and eaten, over and over, hungry, consuming, sated, recycle, repeat.

COME BACK AROUND

Sarina Bosco

Sarina Bosco is a chronic New Englander and hoarder of myths. She works with poetry, fiction, flash fiction, and non-fiction. In her spare time, she also edits manuscripts. Her story 'Soul-Making' appeared in Pulp Literature *Issue 10, Spring 2016*, and we're delighted to share another of her mythic stories with you. This one was shortlisted for the 2020 Raven Short Story Contest.

Come Back Around

When the deer starts talking, it's too far gone.

The ankles are tied, hanging from a pine tree dead from the bottom up, and the blood in the bucket below where the body hangs is steaming in the evening air. He's even sliced the stomach open, all of the organs wet and exposed, but that doesn't stop the voice that comes out of that long, lithe throat covered in tawny hair:

"I just wanted to go to the hickory tree." Said so quietly that the Hunter almost doesn't hear.

He pauses momentarily in wiping off the tool he'd used to gut the animal, before continuing on as if it hadn't said a word.

The Hunter knows exactly what hickory tree the deer is talking about. Half a mile to the south there is a clearing — he knows a man who had a stand there, on the outskirts — and just off-centre in that clearing is an old hickory tree, its bark curling down in thick patches.

The leaves whisper and skitter beneath the Hunter's knees as he stands and presses a palm tight against the spot on his back that feels close to giving out. The deer's body twists slowly on the orange rope he's strung it up with. As it comes around again, a few drops of blood patter into the bucket.

He knows men who cut their deer on the ground, but he likes to see them hanging like this. It makes bleeding the animal easier, too, and he wants a good cupful to attract the coyotes that have been moving in on his property. The rest he will freeze and cube and give to the old woman who takes it daily to fortify her own blood. Half-native and half-crazed, she is, but she pays for it.

He turns back to the deer and, after a glance, reaches inside the gaping cavity, stopping the slow spin. The body jerks with his movements. With a few slices and a grunt, the liver comes free. The sound of it slapping down into the pan he has nearby is loud and ugly.

The deer shivers in a long spasm and seems to come alive again momentarily, though he misses it. He is turned back toward the small clearing he's made in the leaves, working on starting a fire. The Hunter always eats the liver and a piece of the heart before he leaves. It's a tradition his father taught him, and he has carried on with it long after the old man has gone.

"This isn't the season that we see men in the forest," the deer comments quietly. As it comes around again once more, its large eyes seem to be on the Hunter, who avoids the gaze.

The deer is right.

It's early September, and although the mornings have a bite to them now, they are still weeks off from hunting season.

"The early bird gets the worm," the Hunter mutters, shoving errant curls into the edge of his cap. The pan hisses as it heats, and the air is filled with a metallic scent. The deer's body jerks on the rope.

It must take his slip of a sentence as the beginning of a conversation, because it continues talking as he pokes at its liver with a spork:

"There were still hickories on the ground. And there are apples in the orchards now. Just tomorrow I was planning on crossing the brook, going to that place that they don't tend anymore, where children are sometimes."

The Hunter knows this area well, too.

It's the overrun orchard of an older couple who lost their son two seasons back. In late autumn, when the apples spoil, the neighbours are constantly on the lookout for bears drunk on the fruit. His own sister used to sneak down there in their childhood to steal a skirtful at twilight.

"My uncle was a deer," the deer says, which is a ridiculous statement for a gutted deer to make. "Of course, he wasn't a deer right away. He started slipping into it when he was a few months away from dying. I was only two winters old at the time, but I knew it. As soon as he was gone, I could feel him again somewhere else, out in the woods."

The deer pauses here and one ear tilts. Its body has slowed to a stop so that an eye is peering at the Hunter where he sits on his haunches, holding the liver up to cool in the evening air. It already smells like autumn.

"I don't always remember the other lives. I don't know why I'm remembering that one right now."

The Hunter sits straighter, makes a long guttural sound in the back of his throat, and pulls up mucous that he spits into the leaves. The deer's eyelid flutters, lashes so long that any woman would envy them, and it correctly guesses the sound he makes is of disbelief.

"We all come back around," it says.

The Hunter reaches for the black bag he carries and digs around until he finds the knife he was looking for. Without making eye contact with the animal, he comes nose-to-intestines with it and begins to cut at some of the translucent white flesh keeping things together.

"I used to see my uncle in the field when he was a deer. Just no one else realized it was him. Which is strange, don't you think? Maybe as you get older, you forget about these things—how tethered we all are to nature."

With a savage pull, the Hunter loosens the colon and lets the innards spiral out toward the ground. They brush against the deer's delicate chin, and the animal startles at the feel of its own insides.

"There's no need to be so rough."

But the Hunter isn't listening. He's thinking of his sister, the one who used to steal apples, and he's walking a very thin line—almost letting his mind wonder if what the deer is prattling on about might be true, and if she's somewhere out there even now. Maybe in the same woods he stepped into this morning with the intention of leaving with meat and blood and the acrid taste of satisfaction under his tongue.

The Hunter says her name quietly in his mind.

Then he reaches into the throat of the deer, his rough hand feeling out the length of the windpipe, joined by the other holding the knife—one slice high, just under the jawbone, and it's free. The whole mess comes out in one pull.

For a long time the deer is silent, and the Hunter is sure that removing the windpipe has done it. He won't have to listen to its musings anymore, which is good, because he came out here to not think at all; to walk in, kill things, leave.

In all the years of hunting, a deer has never spoken to him. Neither has a turkey or a quail or the dog he'd shot one time on someone's property, a yellow lab that went down like a sack of grain.

"The star grass is blooming at the edges of the stream."

It's said absently, and one glance tells the Hunter that the deer is staring out into the forest. Most likely thinking about those hickory nuts lost in the knotted grass of the clearing.

"I've never seen a second bloom," the deer continues, and the Hunter could respond now. He could tell the deer that occasionally the plant will bloom twice in one season, late the second time.

Instead he spins the body carefully and eyes the thighs, the length of the ears, the sway of the back; what he'd earlier thought to be a seasoned doe he realizes now is an animal maybe only three years old.

"Do you think you'll come back as a deer?"

The question, in a voice light but direct, makes the Hunter stiffen. His right wrist is smeared in blood, and it will make removing the last of the organs dangerous. Which is why, he tells himself, he steps away to rub at the sticky mess with a rag. It isn't fear. It isn't the unwillingness to consider what will come next.

"That would be rather—what is the human word? Ironic?—were you to come back as one of us, to live as one of us. You're the one who's been leaving scent at the stumps and the sumac stands."

That's true. He's been using scent for weeks, trying to get a buck, but it seems they've all moved out of the area for whatever reason. It shouldn't be the case as he's one of the first hunters out, illegally or not.

He'd even tried scenting the coyotes—with a strangely sweet-scented lure that almost always works, piss that the taxidermist collects when his clients won't gut their own animals, even good fresh steak that he'd bought for dinner. But none of it had brought the pack close enough to his poison traps.

The coyotes aren't doing anything reckless, haven't even touched the neighbour's chickens. But he knows a man out in Montana who sells the hides for a good profit to tourists coming into the National Parks. He'll get a good cut if he can ship out a few dozen.

"I knew a doe once," the deer continues, despite the fact that he's starting in on its hide now, cutting careful lines around the ankles, "that saw a man like you. With a hat like that."

This makes the Hunter pause. The hat was his father's, made by his mother, and there were none around that could be its twin; the wool used to make it had come from their own sheep and had been dyed with pokeweed. Stitched with red thread. The ear flaps tie under the chin, but he has them tied up now, over the top of the hat.

"She saw you and followed you for a while. She said she recognized your hat, and that she didn't know why you were out in the woods. She said you didn't go in the woods for a long time after."

The deer says *after* as though it knows what after is, but already it has that faraway gaze in its brown eyes that means it's probably thinking about acorns or black raspberry bushes or sunflowers in some housewife's garden.

But the Hunter knows what the *after* is, and he feels an overwhelming warmth flush his neck and ears before the guilt sets in.

Again he pushes his sister's name from his mind. The deer's tail flickers white against the layered brown surroundings. The rushing sound in his ears is the sound of the brook, the sound of the rocks clacking together, and his sister's head cracking against one when she slipped, farther out than they were supposed to be. Too far for him to carry her back. When he'd come back with his father, she'd been face down in the water.

"Do you think she might have been someone you knew before? Do you ever worry about killing someone you knew?"

The deer doesn't stop chattering as the Hunter stoops and collects his tools, hands shaking so badly that he drops the gutting ring several times, his breath in the cooling air coming out in short puffs. The gun is checked to make sure the safety is well and truly on. Then with jerky movements he unloads it and throws the ammunition out into the leaves and pine needles.

The deer he leaves hanging and turning once more in slow circles. In the rush of trying to leave, the bucket has gone over and blood is darkening the dirt. The guts litter the ground, still wet in the low light—all except for the heart in its casing. This the Hunter clutches in his hand as he hurries out into the trees, trying to get the light voice of the animal out of his head, trying to forget that he'd ever stepped foot here.

SOLSTICE

Melissa Nelson

Melissa Nelson grew up in the Lower Mainland with a horror-movie buff for a mother. Her formative years shaped by monsters, ghosts, and the likes of Jason Voorhees, Melissa now aspires to write something that will keep her mom up at night. 'Solstice' was the runner-up in Pulp Literature's 2021 Bumblebee Flash Fiction Contest.

$\mathcal{S}$OLSTICE

Every winter some star-crossed vagrant finds themselves at our stoop. Sometimes snow-blind, usually numb with hypothermia, they cry when we open the door. Mother peels away their icy clothes, I fetch the warmest quilts, and little brother puts bricks on the fire.

Mother calls them our winter guests. Sometimes they find their way alone; others Father stumbles upon when he is hunting the barren wood. Nestled in, Mother serves them cups of hot broth and I wait for their voice to return to whisper: *What is it like out there?*

Most come from far away, places with department stores and paved roads. This year, our winter guest is from another continent altogether, trying to escape the ghost of his young bride.

She was your age, he says, or maybe a bit older. Consumption, the wicked thing, took her from the world before she got to see it.

On nights when the wind screams, I sneak to the corner of the room to pry up the board behind the basin where I have hidden the book and pencil, a gift he left at the darkest part of winter.

Something to trap dreams with, he said, when I caught him writing in it. When I stared back, he continued, *Dreams like to leave you. If you write them down, they are yours forever.*

Behind the pages he filled, I write down every detail I can remember of our winter guests' stories: general stores they bought supplies in, or rivers they followed into the Rockies.

Our guests are never ours for long. As the New Year looms and snow piles high, they start to worry about moving on. But Mother is persistent—she was a nurse once, before little brother and me. It is one of the two stories we share with our winter guests. The first is fraught with forbidden desire, a young couple driven to the wilderness to escape expectation; the second, the hardship that followed.

It isn't easy, Mother and Father say, *but we find ways to make do with what little we have.* Our winter guests like this. It is an answer to a question they had not thought to ask.

But he did. He thought that isolation was akin to starvation.

There comes a time each year when we wake up to find ourselves trapped with our winter guests. They gaze with saucer eyes at the white walls and then our empty shelves, but Father is an anchor—he was a captain once, before little brother and me. Father's heavy hand on their shoulder, we huddle around our winter guests to give thanks that they found our stoop.

When the thaw comes, Father ventures to the wood to send the winter guest on. Plumes of smoke wave as Mother scrubs the basin and little brother lies in the grass, a stretch of pale winter belly reaching out to greet the sun.

When this thaw comes, I will take the book and see the world they spoke of.

I will scream at the first stoop I find.

THE CANADIAN INVASION

David Perlmutter

David Perlmutter *is a freelance writer based in Winnipeg, Manitoba. His published works include the non-fiction books* America Toons In: A History Of Television Animation *(McFarland and Company) and* The Encyclopedia Of American Animated Television Shows *(Rowman and Littlefield). His short stories and essays can be read on Vocal and Medium. He can be reached on Twitter at @DavidPerlmutt10 and Facebook at DavidKPerlmutterandFriends.*

The Canadian Invasion

JOHN LEMON:

The weirdest part about it all was that we were so popular, eh?

The thing is, none of us meant to become stars. We were just after playin' some rock and roll, and trying to make a living at it, eh?

And me, I probably needed the companionship more than the others, given how I was raised up.

You see Toronto on a map, it don't look like that big a place, but it's right big enough to disappear in and never come out. I got brought up in Etobicoke, which is as far out as you can get and still be in the city. It wasn't the greatest thing, what with my mother out in the psych ward downtown — she went nuts when I was little and never got better — and only my aunt to raise me. So I grew up finding only two things exciting me: the hockey games on the radio on Saturday (naturally, I was always for the Leafs); and then, when I was in my teens, this new-fangled rock and roll came on the scene. None of the local stations would play it at the start, 'cause Toronto was such a *conservative* place, but I could get a good signal on my transistor to the American stations that *did* play it, out in Buffalo and Detroit. Sometimes, on a clear night, I could get WINS from New York City and hear Alan Freed's show. That guy forgot more about rock than most people knew, and it really turned me on.

Next thing you know, I got a guitar and learned how to play, and then I started hanging out on what passed for a music scene on Yonge Street in those days. And that's how I ended up starting what eventually became the Beevers ...

PAUL McADAM:

Back at that time, Montreal was kind of a divided place, even more than it is now. The French people lived in their neighbourhoods, and Westmount, which is where I lived, was all rich English people. Mount Royal, in the centre of the island, was the divider. Nobody told me outright you couldn't go visit the French folks, but you were sort of looked down upon if you were an English person who did.

Not that I cared.

I'd always been into music, since my dad had a sideline playing in a brass band when he wasn't holding down a day job. And, with us being alone at home together, with Mom dead and gone, there was a lot of impetus to do something exciting with my life. That was when, after playing guitar for a while, I started taking it more seriously.

Montreal, back then, was really the entertainment capital of Canada — Toronto was squaresville in comparison — so a lot of big acts came to play the clubs downtown. I could never afford to get in those places, but the English-language radio stations would play their records to promote the gigs. And we were close enough to the American border that we could pick up their radio signals with no trouble at all. Occasionally I might tune in to the local French stations because their music was so spirited you could dance to it without understanding the language. That was the kind of stuff I was trying to copy when I wrote a lot of the bilingual stuff the Beevers cut.

Anyhow, one day there was a party going on in a church parking lot in my neighbourhood, and that was where I met John for the first time. He and his group — the Maples, they were called in those days — had driven up from Toronto because the kids wanted a pop music group, and there weren't any local ones around then. After they were done, I went up and introduced myself, and we connected. I told him I played, and was there any chance they needed somebody new? Actually, there was. They were short one player since one of them had quit. And since I played, was I interested?

Yes, I was. And that was how it all started for me.

GEORGE HAIRSTON:

When you live on the Island — Prince Edward Island, that is — there aren't a huge number of options for you in terms of steady work. Maybe if I lived in Charlottetown, our 'big city', I might have found something regular and stayed. Only I lived on the other end of the Island, where the red clay comes up thick, and there wasn't nothing there in terms of work except planting and digging up potatoes. Which I didn't want to do. Fortunately, being the youngest of four boys, and my three older brothers being okay with working the farm with Dad, I could shift for myself, as far as they were concerned.

I had friends who had moved to Toronto, so I went there. By that time, I had been picking on the guitar my whole life, and everyone was saying I was good enough to be a pro. But not in PEI, I couldn't. There was some spots in Charlottetown I could play, and some other isolated spots in the more remote areas, but not enough to help you make a living at it.

What happened was, once I got to Toronto, I found out that there was this rock band who needed a new player and was having auditions. I went, and that was how I met John and Paul. John was the boss of the group then—like he always thought he was—and he told me to start playing and we'll see if you're good enough. I did, and when I finished, they had their mouths hanging open, like nobody had played that good for them before.

I was not only in, now, I was the *lead* player, with John on rhythm and Paul taking over for their old bass player, who'd just kicked the bucket.

And that's how it stayed until we broke up.

RANGO STARK:

I wasn't exactly what you would call a healthy kid. The year I was born, 1940, the war was on, and everyone was worried that the Nazis was gonna kill us all. My mother more than some others. So, as a result, I got born prematurely, and I kept getting sick so often it seemed that I was in hospital more than school. But, somehow, I survived.

St John's, my hometown, is the main town on the island of Newfoundland—the Rock, as we locals call it. It's in a very strategic part of the Atlantic Ocean, so we got a lot of the traffic coming in from the other side of the pond, and business picked up right quick due to the war. The Americans helped us out a lot that way. Once they entered the war in '41, they set up military installations on the Rock. They liked it so much that they stayed on for some time after the war ended, and nobody was man enough to make them leave.

But that had a side benefit. They brought their culture with them, including their music. Once rock and roll started up in the mid-50s, you could hear it blasting out of the PX at their base at all hours of the day. Some of us didn't like it, but not me. It was wonderful, I thought. And when I discovered that people made their *living*—as in a steady job—doing it, that was it for me. I wanted in.

I couldn't play no guitar like most of the players did in those days, but I had a good feel for rhythm, and, once I got behind a drum kit for the first time, I knew how I was going to be part of the scene.

There were and are plenty of folk music groups on the Rock, but none of them needed a rock-and-roll drummer, so I knew I had to go somewhere else to find that kind of gig.

Since Newfoundland became part of Canada in '49, I knew I could go there and not change my citizenship or nothing. So I went down to Toronto, hoping to find something there.

I started auditioning, with nothing coming at first. But word got round about me sure enough. A couple of bands approached me about taking over for them. Ronnie Hawkins and the Hawks offered me something, and the Beevers something else. Obviously, I went for the Beevers. The key thing was the money: they promised me a steady weekly wage. And that was all I needed to hear.

JOHN LEMON:

By about '62 we'd been making enough noise around Toronto that we had more gigs than we could handle, so we needed a manager. That's when Fred Bartlett took over. His family owned the shop where we were buying instruments, so that made him a natural for the job. Or so it seemed. How were we to know that he knew nothing about cutting good deals and would end up getting us financially screwed, eh?

PAUL McADAM:

Bartlett shopped our demos around, but not many of the few record labels that there were would have us. The only one that was interested in us was Quality, on account of the fact that they were already distributing a lot of the big American rock records in Canada, so having a genuine Canadian rock band on their label wouldn't be much of a stretch. And that was how we met our producer, Gerry Tanqueray.

GEORGE HAIRSTON:

That first session didn't go too well. John and Paul weren't writing too much then, and so we didn't have a lot of decent material to record. And Tanqueray was right mad about that. He read us the riot act about how we should have come in with our act tightened up and decent arrangements and all that. He went on for nearly an hour before any of us could get a word in edgewise.

Finally, he wanted to hear what we had to say in our defence.

I was tired of being lectured, so I told him that, to begin with, I didn't think his tie was on straight enough. There was a pause, and then, boy, did we ever laugh! From that point on, Tanqueray was in our corner.

RANGO STARK:

Up until then, we'd mostly been doing cover tunes, but that was when John and Paul realized that we could make more money if we cut stuff we wrote ourselves. So they started writing and never stopped. Stuff about how love went in Canada, supposedly, and the joys of getting sloppy drunk out in the Canadian Shield, and all that. They had so much going that George and I, even when we came up with something decent, could barely get space for it as a B side!

JOHN LEMON:

We got good at fixing up tunes, Paul and I. I'd start writing a piece, and he'd finish it, or vice versa. Or sometimes we'd be sitting together with our guitars and a couple of beers and work things out right from scratch. Either way, we were luckier than a lot of the bands that came after us. We came up with our own stuff pretty regular-like. Whereas they weren't so good at writing, and had to depend on the Tin Pan Alley gang in New York to give 'em stuff. And it didn't sound as authentically Canadian as ours did 'cause of that. That was our advantage. We weren't a fake American band—we were always Canadian from Eh to Zed.

PAUL McADAM:

The hit run began when 'Lover, Love Me' hit number one in Canada. An American label licensed it to play down there, and it hit number one there, too. Same when it went over to the UK, where they were really starved for rock, it seems, and a lot of other places. After that, we could have released a blooper reel of us goofing off in the studio, and it would have made the top forty, or the top ten, or number one, anywhere in the world.

We were Pandora, and we had opened up a musical box that people really needed. And we were just as surprised as anybody when it happened.

GEORGE HAIRSTON:

That whole time, from '63 to '66, is such a blur to me now. We were always *doing* something: making records, going on tour, playing on TV shows everywhere. And that weird movie, premiering right in downtown Toronto, and us in the middle of the circus! Everyone wanted us. We trusted Bartlett to take care of the money and the legal stuff, and he just told us where and when to be, and we showed up on time, always.

It was probably no wonder we started drinking more often in the few off hours we had. Molsons and Labatts and O'Keefes to begin with, and then more expensive stuff when we could afford it.

RANGO STARK:

John and Paul had started to think that they *were* the band, and that me and George were just add-ons. It got to the point where I couldn't take it anymore, and I let George know. He felt the same way.

That was something we knew about. Newfoundland and PEI have both been exploited plenty economically in the past, with the natives not getting much at all. And usually it was Ontario and Quebec, where John and Paul were from, doing the exploiting.

So George and I were thinking about quitting, and letting John and Paul shift for themselves without a rhythm section.

But then things changed.

Bartlett up and died on us—suicide. And we found out we weren't as rich as we thought we were 'cause he hadn't done the numbers right. I bet he killed himself so we wouldn't have to do that job ourselves.

PAUL McADAM:

We were determined to have control over our career. So we asked Quality if they'd let us set up our own label for our own records, plus make some records for some fellow artists—the Poppy Family, the Bells, Keith Hampshire, folks like that—who we knew could be as big as us with the right kind of marketing. They said all right. As for the name, we were the Beevers, and beavers live in lodges, so calling the label Lodge seemed like the right way to go.

It wasn't just supposed to be about music, though. We had plans for other businesses underneath the Lodge umbrella. I went back home and found this old neglected building on Rue St Catherine that seemed like a good place for a shop. We made it into the Lodge Boutique, with a stock of real Canadian goods——Labatt and Molson beer, Robin Hood flour, McClelland and Stewart books, that kind of stuff.

But we must have rubbed somebody the wrong way, because nobody came to the shop, and it went bust.

GEORGE HAIRSTON:

Turns out we were good musicians but lousy businessmen. Our records on Lodge were just as good, sales-wise, as our Quality ones had been, and our friends had some hits on the label themselves. But we weren't good at translating that into decent equity. Soon we were losing thousands of dollars every day. *Thousands.* We couldn't ignore that——we had to do something.

RANGO STARK:

We'd heard some things about this Alvin Klaw fellow from the States. An accountant, but not a boring one. He specialized in finding money recording artists never knew they made, and getting it for them. The contracts we got were always kind of one-sided and full of legalese, so you never knew everything that was going on under your nose in the deals. Klaw was able to discover that there were millions of dollars being withheld from the artists for the stupidest reasons. Like how many records got broken during the shipping process. How was that *our* fault? *We* didn't *ship* 'em.

It was some of the Canadian acts what came up in our wake that let us know about this. The Rolling Rocks, out of Ottawa, got a big amount from Canadian Decca after Klaw was done with them. Same with the Pegs, out of Winnipeg, after he'd audited Canadian RCA. This was not to be sneezed at.

So we hired him to do an audit on our relationship with Quality. But that was really the beginning of the end.

It had nothing to do with John hanging out too much with his artist girlfriend and starting to record more with her than us, even though a lot of fans think that was the cause. It also wasn't because Paul wanted his own band and to work with his new wife, or because George and I wanted to go solo. That was all gonna happen, anyway; we all had the fame and the resources to do it now.

We just needed an excuse to break up, and Klaw gave it to us.

PAUL McADAM:

I, for one, didn't like Klaw, and didn't want him going over our books. So, once we were clear financially, I told the other guys that, maybe, we needed to stop working together professionally if we were going to save our friendship, which we valued more. And they agreed.

So, really, it was the Klaw that broke the camel's back.

But we still felt the loss. Even when I went and told the press we were done, and they shot those pictures of me, you can vaguely make out tears in my eyes.

JOHN LEMON:

It was bound to happen, eventually. Things had gotten way beyond anything any of us could handle or control. That business stuff screwed us up. If we'd been able to just concentrate on playing tunes, like how we started out playing the clubs on Yonge Street, maybe we would have lasted longer.

GEORGE HAIRSTON:

I knew I did something important — the evidence is all there. Sometimes I did feel like I was just a sideman, being told what to do. But now that I've had to record all on my own these last few years, and still have hits, at least by the standards of RPM magazine, it's not entirely the same as it was with the Beevers.

RANGO STARK:

The most enduring memory I have is how I accidentally came up with the title for our movie. It had no title to start with, and might not have had one but for me. It came out like this. We'd finished shooting for the day, and I'd said goodbye to the others in a way that's fairly customary in Newfoundland. Evidently, the Hollywood types surrounding us weren't familiar with it, 'cause they thought that'd be the perfect title for the flick!

I still don't know what people who have never heard of us and our work, much less Newfoundland, are going to think when they look up what's on TV for the day and come across a movie called *Long May Yer Big Jib Draw!*

COLD BLESSING

Kelsey Hutton

Kelsey Hutton *is a Métis author of speculative fiction from Treaty 1 territory (Winnipeg, Canada). She particularly loves writing historical fantasy, space opera, first-contact stories, and Métis- and Cree-shaped SFF for fellow Indiginerds everywhere. Connect with her at KelseyHutton.com or on Twitter at @KelHuttonAuthor.*

Cold Blessing

The wind had gnawed his skin raw by the time they reached the nun's door, the damp air sunk deep into his bones.

A warm orange glow leaked out of the small cottage into the night. While his daughter bounced about in front of him, immune to winter's bite, he spread his hand out on the door. There, briefly. Not warmth, but a respite from the cold.

Then he shook himself straight and crushed the ice out of his moustache. He wasn't here for respite. He was here so he would never need respite again.

He pulled Maisy in front so she could dart through the door as soon as the nun opened it. "Ready, girl?" he said. "Be good now, hear?"

The child was babbling to herself. She didn't even look at him. Instead she careened a whitish lump about in the air. It was a bit of china clay, covered in silt, that had left streaks all over her hands — and, now that he looked closer, the sleeves of her best dress. And after he'd specifically made the wife wash her up!

"Creep, creep, creep," she chirped and tried to march the clay over his coat cuff.

"Maisy, enough!" He jerked his arm back before it could leave marks on his Sunday suit. He tried to grab it out of her hand, but she twisted away. Her toady eyes bulged further as she laughed.

He unclenched his jaw with some effort. Very well. Let her keep her muck, along with that nose and those teeth and that hair. The fact of the matter was, washing wasn't the problem. His only child would be plain no matter how coarse the brush.

"There'd better be hope for you," he muttered and rapped the door three times. Behind him, the sea roared.

No one denied the nun was an odd one. She wore the robes of a nun, but not the wimple. She never bothered anyone, but the sexton refused to call her Sister. She even had the occasional sweet for a village child.

But most importantly, she had the touch.

The nun edged opened the door. As if on cue, a fierce gale tackled father and daughter from behind. He braced one boot inside the warped doorway as if for balance. "Sorry—so sorry, Sister, to barge right in—Maisy," he hissed, "g'on," and the girl shimmied obediently. The nun gaped, but moved quickly into the gap to block the child from wriggling in.

"Was I not clear?" the nun snapped. "I said no!"

He'd never been this close to her. When she'd refused him twice before, he'd thought her stubborn even for an old nag. But now, up close, she wasn't as worn as he'd remembered: indeed, her black eyes were large and comely, if spaced strangely far apart.

"Hullo!" the child said with a broad smile. He tried to press her forward, but her shoulders were well wedged between the door and its frame. She wiggled one arm free and waved at the nun's face as vigorously as if she'd been across the Thames rather than squished against her skirts. "May we come in, please?"

Briefly, when she looked at Maisy, he thought he saw the nun flinch.

"Please, Sister," he said. "Twilight is long gone. Exposed like this, at night … if nothing else, we must get out of this blistering wind. It is too bitter to turn around now, not without a temporary relief." He saw her hesitate. "Look at the child's fingers! Bone white with cold!" Or clay. "They'll never survive the walk back."

Without quite meaning to, real desperation crept in. He thought of the wife, their plain cottage, their mean little meals. He thought of her fingers, bleeding from twisting dried kelp into logs for the fire. His own were barely sensible anymore, after so many years hauling fish through icy water. Worst of all was that there was no end. Another winter. Another catch. Another night steeped in the stench of fish. "Is this what you want for your only child?" he had demanded of his wife that night, when she wept and begged him not to go. "Don't you want better for her?"

"You're a fool," the nun said finally, but she moved half a step back.

Inside, heady heat seeped into his aching knees. There were a few candles and a kerosene lamp set on a rough-hewn table, offering what light they could. Women's cooking instruments hung from the ceiling, though he couldn't be pressed to name them. Across the back, a long sheet had been strung up with twine, cutting part of the room off from view. The whole cottage smelled thickly of something sweet. Honeysuckle, perhaps. The nun did not latch the door behind them.

"I brought you a present," the child announced, to his surprise as well as the nun's. She held out the pebbly lump of clay. "It's a mouse!"

"Maisy, no——" he started, but the nun held out her hand. Long white fingers wrapped around the gift.

She looked just like the wife when she'd swallowed a fishbone.

"Papa wants you to bless me so someone rich will marry me," the child announced, "even though I'm not pretty like other girls." Then she promptly lost interest.

The nun drew a sharp breath and stepped back.

"Well," the man fumbled, cursing the girl's long ears, "or something that would do her good a bit sooner … a long-lost rich uncle, perhaps?" The nun's expression, if possible, got harder still.

The moment of goodwill was gone. "Get out, both of you!" She nearly shouted.

"The child puts it so bluntly——" he tried. The nun hooked Maisy by the arm.

"No!" She started pushing them out.

"A bit of kindness——"

"Go!"

"Please——"

"I don't bless children like *her*." The nun shoved Maisy past the doorstep into the cold.

"Now wait just a minute, there!" He bristled and planted his feet.

"When you first moved to this village, Sister, we welcomed you, despite not knowing where you come from. We knew your sacred profession, and we saw your kindness for the village children, even the cruel or priggish ones." Bewilderment was creeping into his voice, he could hear. He drew a deep breath to wash it out. "We know you don't like being asked to perform rites, but I seen the change in those children after they come to your attention. You *bless* them! It's true!"

Two bright-red spots appeared in her white cheeks, but he hurried on. "You bless them, and afterwards they marry rich, or get bursaries to fine schools, or … or the like. And, I know" — here he drew himself up to his full height — "I know I'm only a fisherman, but I am a father. As a father, it's my responsibility to make sure my child's prospects, no matter how dim, are well cared for."

He could see it in her eyes, the already-begun shake of her head. She was going to refuse him again. Their life would continue, small, meagre, and hard, like the potatoes they boiled endlessly for tea. "Please, Sister!" he cried. "Try to imagine what it's like, having a child you'd do anything for," he begged. He could well imagine shivering in their damp little cottage all the rest of their days. "Please!"

The nun's mouth twisted into a crooked pink wedge like the snails he used for bait. All three of them, even Maisy, stood frozen in place.

A gale shrieked past them through the little hut's open door. The candlelight wobbled drunkenly, and shadows leapt at each other's throats. For the first time, the fisherman noticed another smell underneath the sweet honeysuckle. His eyes stung with its vinegar sharpness and he blinked repeatedly, wondering how he could have missed it before.

A chill crept up the soft undersides of his arms.

Her shoulders clenched tight, but still the nun wouldn't speak. Then she broke her stare and glanced, quickly, furtively, to the curtained end of her cottage. Only one glance. It was enough.

She pulled them inside, then choked off the wind with a slam of the door.

The nun leaned her face down to the child's. "Maisy, right?" she asked, all trace of her anger washed away. Her smile nearly made her beautiful, and the fisherman's blood suddenly quickened in a way shameful to a man with a wife.

Maisy nodded back with a smile full of crooked teeth.

The nun gently put the gift of clay on the table. He was surprised she'd held onto it this whole time. The nun led the girl towards the back, where a small noise rustled.

"Tell me, child," the nun asked gently. "I am sure your father and mother have taught you to be a good Christian, as parents ought. But do you ever fail in your resolve? Act unkindly towards others?"

"Sometimes," the girl answered.

The nun wrapped her long white fingers around Maisy's arm. "And—" the woman's voice croaked. "How do you make up for it?"

They were at the grimy edge of the curtain now. The woman's eyes never left Maisy's face as she reached behind her. The fisherman, still by the door, shifted on his feet. He better not lose his toes to frostbite on the long walk home.

"Mama makes me do penance," the girl said and touched the nun's cross, swinging gently at eye level.

"Penance . . ." The nun released her breath in a whoosh. "Yes, that's the word." Then she swept back the cloth and the wave of stench hit him like a fist.

He gagged, woozy, but not before he saw what the sheet was hiding, *it*, a body, a child's body. It lay on a bed of slithery fronds, a little boy's body but with wet hair and skin the white-green of a mackerel's belly. And its eyes — the lids — the fisherman looked harder, damning himself as he did — they were shredded as if nibbled by crabs. Only a few tufts of eyelashes were left, and gleaming, pale, under the lids — eyeballs like jelly.

"Maisy!" he called and gagged again with the stench. The girl had buried her face in her hands; to hide from the smell or the sight, he didn't know. Then cold hit his lungs so hard they seized. He clutched his chest. The candlelight flickered wildly, and he could only catch glimpses of his daughter through shifting shadows. Maisy, no longer docile, was yanking away from the nun, her one arm reeling out like a line, almost popping from her shoulder while the nun, that witch, wrestled to keep hold of her hands.

"I would never have chosen a child as sweet as this!" the woman whispered, with a turn in her voice almost pleading, with those eyes so large, like a beetle's. Like a demon's. "But you would not let it go, would you?" She now yelled at the man. "As if you know what makes right wrong and wrong right. As if you know what a parent would do for their child!" And she joined the dead child's hand to Maisy's.

Maisy dropped to her knees. The boy didn't stir. The man broke through whatever had kept a deathly grip on him and ran to his only daughter, but the woman elbowed him in the gut with more force than she had a right to. He dropped to his knees.

Maisy's eyes were as round and unblinking as a pickerel's. She grew still, more still than he'd ever seen her. Steam rose off the children's clasped hands. Maisy's cheek sallowed, and the boy's — the thing's — pinked.

The fisherman couldn't move or breathe. He could only hear his wife's voice in his head. "Don't take her, husband — that woman! The things she does!" She'd warned him, more, begged —

"What are you doing, witch?" he finally gasped. "What kind of blessing is this?"

"This isn't the blessing," the woman bit out. "This——"

He shoved past her, but just as he reached for Maisy the nun grabbed his fingers and twisted them back with that demon strength. He gasped and froze, and she caught him like that, her grip tight, his joints screaming, their hands in mid-air beside the children's.

Her face moved right up to his. Her words tumbled over each other like spume. "I could take it back," she gasped. He started to agree, but she cut him off. "But my son! The sea swallowed him, ripped him out of my hands, after we'd run away so they wouldn't rip us apart, after we thought we were safe. The waves spat him back out, almost the same, almost, but he was so cold."

"This is your child?" the man bleated. A nun, with a swollen belly. Spreading her legs for someone other than God.

Her lips twisted again, and her beetle eyes narrowed. "Yes," she hissed. "I can see you judging me already. But I tried." Her voice rose to a panicked pitch. "I tried to treat with the Lord! I did! But the Lord wouldn't listen. I had to make a deal with someone ... else." She shook his arm, and a sheen of tears fevered her eyes. "My boy was so cold. How could I leave him like that?"

He couldn't rip his eyes away from hers. "Now I keep him warm, for a while at a time, until one day, He"——she broke eye contact only long enough to look at the floor, *through* the floor——"will bring my boy back to me."

The fisherman shook his head, back and forth, eyes tearing, unable to blink.

"It's only a little warmth from the girl," the woman insisted. "She'll live on normally, most of the time. And I can bless her.

I have the touch. This isn't the blessing, don't you see, but after … I can make her life easier. Make your life easier. That at least. Is that so wrong?"

The vision engulfed him. The three of them in a London house far from the stink of fish. His moustache silvered, but full. The wife was smiling in a rich red dress with pearl beading, looking almost like when she was young. Maisy, grown-up now, sat the closest to the fire and nodded to no one in particular. She was wrapped in shawls. A footman interrupted gently to bring them tea. Cranberry scones, and not a potato in sight.

Loosened pressure around his fingers brought him back, and he yelped at the sudden lack of pain. "Should I still bless her?" The nun, witch, demon, he didn't know, now stroked his trembling fingers. "Should I bless her?" she pressed, but softly, her voice like velvet. "Or should I take everything back?"

It wasn't Maisy's life. The witch wasn't looking to take her life. Only a little heat.

Suddenly he could blink again. He closed his watering eyes and nodded, sharply, once. "Do it," he whispered.

All four of them fell back, released. He caught Maisy and finally pulled her away from the corpse. She shook once violently, then in small tremors. Her eyes wouldn't focus. "Cold, Papa," she whispered. "I'm cold."

The witch stroked the dead thing's rosy cheek. He never opened those jellied eyes, thank God. The fisherman touched Maisy's skin. It was ice.

He took her tiny hands, fingernails purple, and rubbed them between his own large palms. The woman got up and reached for something in the cupboard.

He had to try three times before he could get the words out. "How long does it last?"

The woman spat out a "Huh!" She was back with a bowl. She dipped her fingers, mumbled some words, and sprinkled water on Maisy's hair. He thought it holy water until he smelled the brine.

Maisy's hands wouldn't warm up. My God, he thought. My God.

The woman finally looked at him again. "I do my penance," the creature said instead of an answer. "She will marry a banker, one so rich he twists dollar bills to light his cigars." She sat back on the bed of fronds, beside her boy, and turned her back to the man and his daughter.

Maisy trembled and looked past him with drained eyes. He remembered the other blessed children, the cruel ones. With the luckiest of fortunes … and dull eyes, and clammy skin.

He choked as he picked up Maisy. He remembered the lump of clay and swiped it from the table. "Play with this, child." He pressed it repeatedly into her hand, but it only fell from her numb fingers.

The fisherman held his daughter in his arms, chin tucked in, and turned to go. "I wouldn't have taken from her," the nun said suddenly. "I tried so many times to resist."

He spat in the direction of the fallen nun. "Spare me your piety," he managed.

She turned her head slowly, then rose, and he swallowed this one act of defiance like bile. "You still judge," she said. "Even though you know now how easy it is to make one decision, then another, then another, and suddenly you're making a terrible choice you never thought you'd make." She was in front of him now, leaning in close, so close his stomach curdled. "But remember this, fisherman," she whispered. "At least I chose my child."

He turned his back on the witch with a halo of lantern light. He took the first step home through the snow, then the second.

He held Maisy close. Her small frame was already exhausted from shivering. She slipped purple fingers, still streaked with clay, under the cuff of his sleeve. "It creeps, Papa," she whispered. "The cold, it creeps."

ATTEMPTED MURDER

Leslie Wibberley

Leslie Wibberley lives in a suburb of Vancouver, Canada, with her amazing family and an overly enthusiastic cocker spaniel. She writes across a wide range of genres, age groups, and narrative styles. Her work is published in multiple literary journals and anthologies, including seven editions of Chicken Soup for the Soul and the Bram Stoker—nominated Not All Monsters, and has placed first in the Writer's Digest *Annual Writing Competition* and in their *Popular Fiction Awards*. You can reach her at lawibberley@gmail.com.

*A*TTEMPTED *M*URDER

I peered through the windshield of our ancient Buick. Dark clouds of birds filled the twilight sky in an undulating stream, wings beating with singular intent as they headed to their nightly roosting spots. Many more perched on rooftops, along wires and fences, and in the trees that lined the street.

Blue-black demons disguised as crows.

Goosebumps erupted across my skin and a cold sweat trickled down my back. My breathing changed tempo, becoming shallow and rapid. The muscles in my chest tightened as my heart rate accelerated. Nausea danced through my belly.

Holy shit, Agnes, pull yourself together. You've been driving through this same neighbourhood twice a week for two months. Get over it.

I wondered if it was finally time to see someone about this phobia of mine.

Reading my mind, Frankie, my fifteen-year-old daughter, asked, "What do you suppose they're thinking about?"

"The crows?"

"Yeah. They seem so intent. They must be thinking about something important." From the corner of my eye I could see her hands waving expansively at the front windshield and passenger-side window.

The roosting birds stared down at us, their beady eyes filled with malevolence as the Buick limped along the street.

"Probably about who they should murder."

Months earlier, when our route to Frankie's new dance class had led us through this unsettling phenomenon, she'd named this section of the city *Birdtown*. Every evening as twilight approached, it welcomed thousands of the feathered fiends.

"Mom, get serious."

"I am serious. They freak me out. Always have; always will."

"They're just birds, not messengers from hell."

"Can't prove that by me. I hate them. Ever since that evil black shit dive-bombed me and almost pecked my eyeball out." I tapped the small jagged scar above my left eyebrow.

Frankie snorted. "Get over it, Mom. That was over thirty years ago. And besides, one attack doesn't mean all of birdkind is out to get you."

I raised a brow. "Don't be so sure. They know I hate them. It's like when you meet someone and immediately decide you don't like them. They can tell. That's why they dislike you back. Well, that's what it's like with me and birds: a mutual hating."

I'd been twelve, out raking leaves in our front yard. A crow grabbed a baby robin from the nest in the blue spruce at the back of the lawn. The baby bird fell from the crow's grasp, landing on the grass by my feet. Horrified, I bent to rescue the tiny thing, cradling it in my hands. The crow swooped, claws outstretched, and attacked me. I dropped the baby so I could swat at the damn crow. It kept pecking at my hands until it drew blood.

Then the evil shit dove at the back of my head, clawing at my hair. I flung the rake and managed to hit the crow. It flew away and landed in the tree. I wiped at the blood pouring down the back of my hands and backed up towards our porch, gaze fixed on the crow all the way. Seconds later, the damn thing erupted from the tree and flew at my eyes. I ducked my head and covered my face with my arms, but not before a claw ripped the skin above my left eye.

My dad heard me screeching and ran out, brandishing a broom. He scared the crow off. Mom cleaned off my face and hands. Took them over an hour to settle me down. Dad told me it was just a random act and nothing to worry about.

I never believed him.

Mom brought me a cup of peppermint tea, and she and I sat together by the front window, staring at the tree, the robin's nest, and the two birds doing battle.

The mother robin tried valiantly to defend her nest, but the crow was too large, too powerful. In the end, it tossed every damn one of those babies onto the ground. It didn't even use the nest. The next day I borrowed Dad's pellet gun.

I was a good shot.

"Mom?"

I jumped. Lost in my memory, I hadn't been paying attention to Frankie.

"What?"

"The car is making a weird noise."

Gasping and choking, the Buick's engine sounded like a drowning man struggling to breathe. The car shuddered for a moment, the steering wheel vibrating beneath my hands. Damn.

We couldn't afford another repair bill, not if I wanted to keep Frankie in dance and have enough left over to buy groceries. Trying to sound unconcerned, because Frankie already worried enough about things she couldn't change, I said, "It's probably just a bad tank of gas. It can make the engine stutter."

"Are you sure?"

I patted her hand. "Yes, I'm sure. Stop worrying." My girl took after me in that regard. We were both blessed with the worry gene.

To take her mind off the ailing car, I returned to my bird bashing. "And as for those birds, they're demons, every damned one of them. Nothing but a blight on the world."

Bristling with indignation for her feathered friends, Frankie said, "You can't judge an entire species because of the actions of a single crow."

"I can, and I do."

From the corner of my eye, I saw Frankie toss her head. Her hair rippled like a freaking shampoo commercial. Damn, my girl was beautiful.

"How can I possibly be related to you?" Her tone was snarky, but love for me was clear in the smile she flashed.

Frankie loved birds. All birds. From the time she was a little girl, she'd been asking for a pet bird—a parrot specifically. Like there was any chance in hell of that happening. I told her when she moved out on her own, she could have twenty parrots, but she shouldn't expect any visits from me.

"Birds are beautiful and mysterious. And they can *fly*. Imagine being able to soar across the sky and ride a thermal, spiralling up to the edge of the world? That must be the most incredible sensation."

I shrugged, her passion almost, but not quite, drawing me in.

"And have you ever seen a murmuration?"

"No, and neither have you."

"Mommm." She drew the word out like a Slinky. "I'm trying to make a point here. And besides, I've watched videos."

"Just bugging you." I glanced at her. Love for this child of mine expanded inside my chest until it was all I could do not to reach over and squish her in a hug.

A dreamy smile spread across her freckled face. "It's an amazing sight. All those birds flying together in perfect synchronization, like a single organism with a shared brain. I think this roosting behaviour is the same sort of thing. They all end up in the same place every single night, at the same time, because they're all connected."

"Why the sudden interest? We drive by these bloody birds every week."

"I'm doing a project on collective consciousness for school."

"Collective what?"

"It's about how a group can share a single belief system or the same knowledge base."

"I'm pretty sure your teacher meant for you to study humans, not birds."

"But birds are a million times more interesting than people." She leaned back in her seat and stared out the window, lost in her thoughts.

I smiled and shook my head. Frankie was a deep thinker, brilliant and far-seeing, but a little odd. She got that from her father. I was the practical one in our family. As a bookkeeper, I put the bread on the table. My husband wasted his days writing, convinced he was going to write a best-seller and make us rich. To date, he'd only published a few short stories. When things were going well for him, he was charming. When they weren't, well, let's just say he wasn't quite as charming. I told myself if he'd ever raised a hand to Frankie, I would've packed our bags and blown out of there.

But he'd never touched her, preferring me as his punching bag. And so I stayed, frozen into inertia by my own cowardice.

Frankie was the only good to come from our marriage. My sweet girl deserved a mother with a backbone, not a spineless jellyfish like me.

I eased off on the gas and turned the final corner of our trip. The trees lining Johnson Street, where the dance studio was located, were even more densely laden with birds. My pulse accelerated again.

Oblivious to my distress, Frankie leaned forward and gazed out the windshield at the birds. "I think they communicate with each other through telepathy."

"Telepathy?"

"Yeah. Like they're psychic and communicate via thoughts."

"I can't say that's the most reassuring of concepts. If they're psychic, maybe they all knew that crow, and they're sitting up there, plotting revenge."

We pulled into the parking lot outside the studio. I always parked the car as close to the front door as I could get to ensure our trip inside was as short as possible.

No point in tempting fate.

She leaned over and kissed me on the cheek. "Maybe you should stay in the car, then." She smiled and grabbed her bag from the back seat. "Just in case."

"Cheeky child." I shot her a grin. "I wasn't coming in anyway. I've got some work to do. I'm heading out to Starbucks. See you at seven thirty."

I frequently spent Frankie's class time at the coffee shop. It was a nice peaceful environment for work, and they had free wi-fi. Although it was only five blocks away from the studio, I always drove. No damned way I was walking through those birds.

I slipped the Buick into reverse and cranked the wheel, backing out of the stall. Something crunched with a sickening pop. Worried I'd hit someone's pet, I slammed the car into park and jumped out. There was a flattened pile of black feathers and branches interlaced with pieces of grass, just under the rear wheel. I squatted down, surprised to see the remains of a bird's nest and what was obviously a few baby birds. Crows, by the look of it. I wondered how on earth a nest had ended up in the parking lot. Wind must have blown it down.

Disgusted, I wiped my hands against my slacks and climbed back in the car.

Good riddance, if you ask me.

I pulled out of the parking lot, and the engine shuddered again. Fortunately, after a few choking gasps, it smoothed out. I exhaled a puff of relieved air.

The street lights blinked on as I headed down the narrow, tree-lined street. I passed Chin's Corner Store on the way, reminding myself to stop for a jug of milk. A few more blocks down the street, directly across from Spencer Park — a small green space with a duck pond and playground — the Buick gave a mighty wheeze and died.

"Fuckity fuck, fuck, fuck." I managed to reef the wheel hard enough to steer the car to the side of the road before it rolled to a stop. I turned the key, but the only response was a brief, wheezy whine. A second attempt produced only silence. The radio still worked, as did the lights, so it wasn't the battery. Starter? Nah, that wouldn't have explained the sputtering engine.

Shit. I didn't need this. I fumbled in my purse for my cell phone, digging through the black hole that was my bag.

That's when the first crow hit the windshield. The bird seemed stunned but shook itself off and perched on the wiper blade, staring at me with its black devil's eye.

My hand found the phone, and I pulled it out. The stupid thing was dead. Why did I never remember to charge it? And of course, I didn't have a cord to plug it into the car's outlet.

Two more birds hit, one on the side window, the other joining the first on the windshield.

Okay, this was getting bat-shit weird. Why the hell were these birds attacking a car?

Because you're trapped inside, and they know it.

"You're losing it, Agnes," I berated myself. "You probably just drove by their nest or something."

A cloud of birds descended on the car, flying at the windows from all sides. Their blue-black wings beat at a frenetic tempo against the glass.

I screamed, unable to control the hot rush of terror that coursed through my body. Instinctively, I raised my arms to protect my face, whispering "go away" over and over, like some kind of moronic parrot.

It took a moment to register that the beating wings had stopped. I dropped my arms. They were gone. Other than a few disgusting smears on the windows, there was no sign they'd ever been there. I scanned the streets. Birds still roosted in the trees, and on the power lines and roofs, but they sat calmly, as if they'd never left.

What the hell?

The thumping bass in my chest made it hard to think. I pulled in a deep breath and pushed the panic away. I glanced at my dead phone again. What was I supposed to do now? Turning, I could see the lights from the corner store in the distance, a mere three blocks back. I could just walk there and use their phone. No big deal.

Sure, Agnes. No big deal. And in just over an hour your daughter will walk out of that dance studio and find your bones picked clean in the middle of the street.

I tried the key one more time, with the same result. I turned off the headlights to save the battery. Ducking my head, I peeked up at the birds through the windshield. I swear they were all watching me. Waiting for my next move.

The sun dropped toward the horizon, turning the sky a saturated cobalt. The trees that lined the street cast elongated shadows against the sidewalk. Every damned one looked exactly like a bird flying with outstretched claws. Didn't do much for my state of mind.

I checked my watch, surprised to see it was already 6:50. I only had forty minutes to figure this out before Frankie's class ended. I rolled the window down halfway and stuck my head outside to test the waters, so to speak.

The trees exploded with the rustling of a thousand wings, and raucous screams pierced the air. A few birds took flight. Frantic, I rolled the window up again. A crow smashed against the glass just as it sealed up tight.

As if a signal had been given, birds lifted off the trees and roofs and wires and descended on the car in a swirling black cloud.

A strangled scream ripped through my throat, and I peed a little.

Birds bounced off the windows, the hood, and the doors in a thunderous avian rainstorm.

I screamed again and ducked down in the seat, this time pulling my jacket over my head.

Like before, it took a moment to realize the flailing of bird bodies against the car had stopped. Tentative, I lifted my head and peered outside. My stomach flipped at the sight of a hundred tiny, star-shaped fissures spread across the windshield.

The glass wouldn't withstand another onslaught.

They were going to get in.

I was going to die.

Damn It, Agnes. Just once can you not be such a fucking coward? You are not going to sit in this car and die like a loser. Get your ass out of this car.

Twisting in my seat, I stared back at Chin's store.

At forty-seven, I was still in pretty decent shape. To save gas, I biked ten kilometres to and from work every day, and I ran at least three times a week. I was no sprinter, but surely I could make it three blocks before they caught me.

Couldn't I?

Doubt crept in as I imagined the beaks and claws tearing at my flesh. I shifted, noticing the damp spot at my crotch. Embarrassment flashed, quickly replaced by resignation. A little pee was the least of my worries.

Okay. It was now or never. I yanked on the door handle and jumped out, blasting down the sidewalk with heart in throat.

The birds hit me seconds later, a mere twenty feet from the car. Waving my hands, I smashed at them, pushing my way back through a writhing mass of feathers and claws and beaks to the car. I yanked the door open and clambered inside. Two crows made it in before I could shut the door. They flew straight for my face, so I grabbed my bag and slammed it against their bodies, over and over, until they were nothing but a pulpy mass of blood and feathers.

Blood dripped down my own face, obscuring my vision. I swiped it away, and looked out the window.

Time froze at the sight of the birds sitting on the car. Every centimetre of the Buick's hood, and likely the roof and trunk as well, was covered in birds. Rows and rows of birds. Their eyes burned into my own.

Waiting.

I glanced at my watch: 7:25.

Oh my God. Frankie.

If I didn't get back in time, she was going to come looking for me. Whenever I was late, she just wandered down to the coffee shop and joined me for a drink before we headed home.

The birds were going to attack her, too.

Shit. I had to go back out there.

Fear rushed, burning through my veins, thick and hot. No. I couldn't do it. They'd peck my eyes out, and then rip my body into strips of mangled flesh. I could see the whole scenario flashing before me like a slow-motion horror movie.

And then they'd start on Frankie.

Fuck. Why was I such a coward? I was her mother, damn it. My job was to protect her.

Think, Agnes. You're an intelligent human being. These are birds. You can outsmart them.

I breathed out. Of course I could. Hadn't I read somewhere that crows and ravens were as smart as apes? Shit, shit, shit. I needed a plan.

Five minutes later, I was still sitting in the car, staring at the birds.

Armour. That's what I needed, a suit of armour—something to ward off the beaks and claws.

The idea came to me in a flash. I dug in the back seat, trying to ignore the murderous stares of the birds that covered the car, I found an old blanket, my bike helmet and gloves, and a warm jacket I always left in the car in case the Buick broke down.

A quick glance at my watch confirmed I'd run out of time: 7:37.

I crammed the helmet on, pulled on the jacket and gloves, and grabbed a pair of sunglasses from the glove box. I slipped them on and opened the door.

Prepared to do battle for my girl.

The birds descended the moment my feet hit the pavement, but I hunched over and struggled to the back of the car where my bike rack was. Sharp claws sliced through my coat. Wings beat against the helmet, but I kept going. Grabbing the pump from the bike, I waved it back and forth over my head, crashing it into the birds.

And then I put my head down and ran.

"Mom!" Frankie's shrill cry rang out, and I lifted my head. My girl was running towards me.

"Go back," I yelled. "Get inside, and I'll join you."

"No, I'm not leaving you."

Stupid girl.

I leapt at her, flattening her against the pavement, wrapping her in the blanket, covering her body with my own, kissing her cheek, crying, praying.

The birds pelted my back, ripping my jacket, tearing at my jeans, drawing blood.

And then they stopped.

We lay motionless, my baby girl and I, not daring to move, not daring to hope that it was over.

One minute, two, three — and still nothing.

Frankie grunted. "You're kind of heavy."

I lifted my head. The birds were gone, returned to their roosts. Rolling off Frankie's slender body, I asked, "Are you okay?"

Her voice trembled as she said, "I think so."

We sat up, me bleeding from multiple stab wounds, Frankie shivering, and both of us in shock. We stared up at the birds peering down at us. I was afraid to move, to provoke another attack. Five minutes passed. Not a single car drove by while we cowered on the sidewalk.

Why the hell had they stopped? Because they recognized a friend in Frankie? Or maybe they thought I'd learned my lesson.

I supposed I'd go to my grave never knowing the answer.

I pulled Frankie to her feet, still watching the birds. But they made no move to attack.

Frankie started shaking and sobbing, sputtering through her tears. "I thought you were going to die."

I brushed her hair back and kissed her forehead. "Me? Nah. I'm too stubborn to die." Then I wrapped her in my arms, filled with an odd sense of peace.

We took a cab home, packed our bags with the bare essentials, and walked out the door.

MY NAME IS PHILOMENA

Robin Malcolm

Robin Malcolm is native to Seattle, Washington, transplanted to West Africa, where she writes curriculum and resources for local schools and churches. She has published two books in her professional capacity, but fiction is her therapy. She loves telling honest stories grounded in living, breathing places. Her story 'The Bumblebee's Daughter' appeared in Pulp Literature Issue 24. Robin is a two-time winner of the Surrey International Storyteller's Award, and she is currently working on two novels and a memoir of her life in Africa.

$\mathcal{M}$Y NAME IS PHILOMENA

In the days of the trapping old-timers and prospecting gold miners, when Seattle was a boom town full of timber barons drinking beside lumberjacks, when scoundrels were thick as flies and even upstanding citizens were known to rot like meat in the sun, there was a girl who did not know her name. That girl was me.

I rather liked to think it might be something fancy like Anastasia or Katerina, but it did not matter because nobody ever addressed me by name. The crooked fur trader spat "girl" through his rotten teeth when he was sober, and nothing at all when he wasn't. Prior to his mouldy cabin under the old-growth forest, I have no memory at all. Later, those who recognized my face upon their fair streets sometimes called me "otter girl" for the sea-otter pelt I wore around my neck.

I did not like this title. I was quick to plant my feet and raise my voice to correct them. "My name is Beatrice," I told the shopkeeper who gave me scraps from his dinner table in exchange for sweeping the walk each day. And "I am Alberta" I told the laundress who chased me from her sheltered doorway.

The city was different then — a wilderness not yet tamed, only bartered with. The forested hills rose up out of Puget Sound like a bull in a bathtub, and people clung to its side like ticks. An oxcart road ended at the top of First Hill above the sawmill, and, from there, logs were greased and skidded down to Mr Yesler's steam-powered sawmill against a tide flat on the bay. The smell was outrageous on Skid Road, as was to be expected when the city's sewage, dumped straight into the bay, was generously returned with the incoming tide. The muck sucked and puckered at my feet as I stepped up onto the planking of the mill porch.

"Work today, Mr Horton?"

"Penny a day, same as always. Buckets over there, girl." He turned back to his work.

"Eugenie," I told him. "My name is Eugenie." But my voice was lost under the shrieking of the saw blade.

I joined the queue of a dozen others, and when it was my turn, I took a tin bucket in each hand and filled them with the sweet sawdust. Then I stepped out into the horse-dunged streets in search of new potholes to fill. The never-ending rain ensured there were always plenty.

On my third trip of the day, I turned a corner and discovered the swinging body of a boy. He was not much older than I, and hanged for some petty crime. The rope that held him by the neck creaked on the tree branch, and I could not stomach to look at his purpled face, so I darted down an alley.

It was there that I came upon the dog. He was sunk in a quicksand pothole, only his head showing at ground level, and he whined like a rusty gate pulled at its hinges, frantically working his shoulders. The muck and sawdust held him fast. Indeed, the mire had swallowed entire horses, and had I not happened upon him that day, he surely would have perished.

I did not mind so much the filth he left on my clothes, only wanting to keep the otter pelt clean, and once he was set upon solid ground again, I worked the clumps from his thick fur before they dried hard as cement. He thanked me open-handedly by lying down upon his wolfish paws and closing his eyes.

Living things need a name, given to them by someone who cares to know them. As I pondered what this one's name might be, a pair of well-heeled strangers passed by. The dog curled back a black lip and growled, but I tutted and patted him. "They pretend not to see me," I reassured him. "No danger." Nevertheless, I named him Sawtooth, for he was incisive.

Sawtooth became my permanent companion. At my hand during the day, he chaperoned my spiralling path up the streets as I searched for potholes to fill, and down again to the mill with empty buckets. When day became night, we scavenged the back doors and trash heaps for food, sharing equally. And if the Occidental Hotel had discarded table scraps, or if Mr Kensley had been so careless as to jettison a perfectly good pig knuckle behind his butcher shop, Sawtooth knew it. He was magic, that dog, and we kept each other as singular friends.

Meanwhile, the city boomed around us. The thousand-year-old fir sentinels were felled and skidded to the bay. Brick buildings with arched windows and ornamented corbels rose up between the derelict clapboard buildings, so like the ladies in the street trying to keep their silks and lace out of the mud. There was talk of an electric trolley to climb the hill. But still the incoming tide backflushed twice a day, spouting out the city's toilets. The rain fell as it always did, and the carts and horses kept coming, and all the sawdust in the world couldn't keep the potholes filled.

Everything changed one fine day in June, when Mr Berg left a pot of glue on the fire at the cabinetmaker's shop and it boiled over. I smelled the smoke early in the afternoon. I gave it little mind, but Sawtooth began to nudge and push, southwards out of the city. I disregarded his suggestions, thinking perhaps he had only scented a stray chicken. The fire bells were distant, after all, and down an alley I spied treasure—a bit of discarded flannel fabric. But the dog blocked my way.

"What is wrong with you, you great beast? It'll only be another shanty gone up by the cook's carelessness. Get out of my way." Yet the hard-headed lout held fast, not letting me pass and having the gall to threaten me with those saw teeth whenI dared try. Even as I berated his odd behaviour, flames began to erupt across the alley behind him. A wall of heat parched my face, and the fire unfurled, spreading tendrils from building to building, feasting on an entire city built of timber.

I abandoned the flannel and my buckets, racing back through the streets. The smoke burned thick in my chest, and I covered my nose and mouth with the otter pelt. Sawtooth coughed and shook his head, but he never checked, herding me with his full weight so that I was a sheep to his will.

When I reached Skid Road, I pulled up short. There, the young clerk at Mr L P Smith's jewellery shop was frantically piling silver and other valuables in the street. Even as the upper floors of his building burned, he reeled back into his shop, a handkerchief to his face, to retrieve more goods. I watched, hesitating to approach too close to this stranger of unknown character. But when he bent deeply at the waist and coughed as if he were turning inside out, my indecision became resolve. I ran around the corner where the coalman's donkey cart was parked in front of the public house. The abandoned donkey was coated with seafoam sweat, his eyes rolling about, and he balked when I tried to lead him. I knew this beast, though, having long ago named him Steadfast. Soft words and softer hands soon quieted him, and he consented to help.

I said nothing but took over the young clerk's task of moving silver candelabras, pocket watches, and velvet-lined boxes from the shop to the cart. The man made no response to my efforts, only sat on the planking, tears etching white tracks in the soot on his smooth cheeks. It was fortunate that he rallied just as the shop was emptied, however, for I felt my own eternal rest closing in. He motioned me to sit upon his salvaged wealth and led the donkey away from the ravenous flames—a stumbling man with a stumbling beast, trying not to tread on the fleeing rats.

From the top of the hill, and away from the conflagration, we surveyed a world painted a hellish red, inhaling the ash and burning creosote. The fire brigades battled and volunteers worked, but the wood hydrants burned, the tide was out, and for once, there was no rain.

After what seemed an eternity, the clerk came to himself. He cleared his throat and spoke with a rasp. "To whom do I owe such a great thanks? What is your name?"

Surprised by the question, I was at a loss to answer. Nobody had ever asked my name. Beside me, Sawtooth licked his blistered paws, saying nothing—a fine time for him to turn taciturn, compelling me to speak. I cast around for a suitable answer. A discarded newspaper tumbled up the street as if it too were escaping the underworld below, and a name on the headline caught my eye. "My name is Grover Cleveland," I replied.

The clerk tried to hide a smile but failed, and a peculiar sheepishness swirled in my stomach like a bit of bad clams. I dismounted the cart, but before I could flee, the man spoke again. "Thank you, Miss Cleveland. And thank you to your noble dog as well."

By the wee hours of the morning, the flames had finally yielded to darkness. Thirty square blocks of the city had burned. The shacks, shanties, and fine wood homes were gone. The brick ladies were stripped back to their underclothes. Skid Road smouldered for days, and the sawmill was nothing but ash.

The city wasted no time in rebuilding. New brick ladies rose out of the mud almost as quickly as they had burned. So quickly, in fact, that they were caught unawares by the plan to solve the sewage problem by raising the levels of the streets. Fifteen-foot retaining walls went up along every block. In less than a year, storefronts doing daily business suddenly found themselves at the bottom of a deep ravine, with the carriages and trolleys clanging by overhead. Ladders were, of course, provided for patrons.

Sawtooth and I, deprived of our previous employment, soon found a new vocation. "Carry your parcels up the ladder, sir?" I called out, day after day, standing down in the sunless depths of the ditch. "Penny a trip, ma'am."

One morning under a rare glowing autumn sun, a carriage door opened, and a tightly corseted woman with a jiggling décolletage descended. Beneath a wide hat, her mouth was painted bawdy red, and she looked me up and down as if I were a bolt of plain muslin, before hooking a claw under my jaw. "You're a lovely little thing beneath that filth." Her honeyed smile sat on top of her face. "Come work for me. I can take you out of the gutter. Give you a home. Plenty to eat."

Even had I been tempted, Sawtooth pacing behind me was enough to set the first warning bells ringing. But it was when she reached out and stroked the pelt about my neck that I was undone. "No one will trouble you, girl. Even the police are my clients."

I pulled my otter away from her oily fingers and met her gaze without deference. "My name is Helga," I said.

It was the ugliest name I could think of.

One evening, in the damp press of winter, Sawtooth and I had settled behind the blacksmith's shop. It was a rare clear night, the wind driving an ache into my ears, but the brick wall behind the forge radiated warmth. Buried beneath Sawtooth's arctic coat, I slept, sheltered and dry, until his rumbling growl pulled me from sleep. The hairs on the back of his neck bristled, and, ever so stealthily, his black lip curled back to reveal his eponymous teeth. I sat up, peering into the darkness, and gradually made out the charcoal form of three men. They wore the straight backs and thin beards of youth, and as they advanced, starlight revealed their dapper clothing, cockled and soiled. A bitter stink blew off of them, as if they had spent all their allowance on whiskey and it was oozing out their pores.

The smell was a living memory which quickly laid rough hands on me. The old fur-trader's rough hands. The smell on his breath. *Hold still, girl.* My knees buckled and my bladder loosened. "Swine!" I called out. "You smell like a seal carcass rotting in the sun!"

"Get rid of the dog and you can have the girl first," one said to the other. His exhaled breath curled like a ghoul in the darkness.

It took only one intruder raising a rod to launch Sawtooth to duty. He leaped at the offender's throat with a snarl, and the man fell, clattering backwards into a pile of scrap iron. His companions, momentarily stunned by the swiftness with which judgement had fallen on their drunken endeavour, called out terrified curses and staggered away. I picked up a rock and threw it at their vanishing forms, but my limbs trembled, and my aim was poor. "My name is Courage," I whimpered.

Sawtooth's malediction upon their comrade grew silent, and he sat on cool haunches. It was only then that I realized with rising horror that the body of a young heir to the city lay at my feet, dead not from the attack of those saw teeth, but from the strike of his skull against the edge of a broken ploughshare. His blood pooled hot at my feet, and a cold crept into my bowels.

Hearing the awful creak of the hangman's rope, I thought only to get far away. I had nowhere to go where daylight wouldn't expose me and no one to turn to who wouldn't betray me. I only knew to run. Sawtooth ran vigilant by my side. Together we ran until I was gasping for breath and could run no more. At last, I retreated into a narrow doorway, my teeth chattering.

Surprisingly, the door yielded to the weight of my body. Instead of an ascending stair, I found a downward tread. Where it went, I could not tell, for it seemed to plunge into a pool of ink, but the darkness whispered safety. With my hands tracing the brick wall for guidance, I submerged.

Soon the darkness parted like velvet curtains to reveal an emaciated light, as if a single lantern were burning far-off, down a corridor. Passageways branched off in all directions. A roulette wheel chattered down a side corridor, followed by an explosion of raucous laughter. The sound tumbled about with the smell of mildew and dust and the sticky ammonia smell of opium, funnelled in from another corridor. But once my racing heart slowed, I recognized the bricked-up doorways and signage in between: 'The Jericho Mission', 'Sam's Drug Store', and 'Steam Baths, 10 cents'. The city had been slowly closing over the ravines with new sidewalks at street level. How odd it was, this old street I recognized, now underground beneath the petticoats of the brick ladies.

My sweat dried cold as I continued to wander. Rounding a corner, I collided with a wall of warm flesh. His hands fell upon my shoulders, and I choked back a scream of flailing alarm. "No! Go to the stockyards if you want a warm body!"

Startled as I was, the man was startled too. "Pardon, Miss … oh … Are you unwell? I mean you no harm." He raised his hands in surrender. "No harm. Plenty down here who will, though. If you'll come with me, I'll show you where you can sleep safely."

I examined the stranger. He was tall and thin, wearing shirtsleeves rolled at the elbow, and braces. His face was in shadow, so that I could only see the outline of a great moustache curled up at the ends. Doubts crawled over my skin like lice, and I scratched at them as I considered. There could be peril in his offer. On the other hand, Sawtooth, the faithless beast, had failed to warn me of the stranger's approach, only wagged his ridiculous tail. With a scratch of thanks between his ears, I resolved to gamble my life on my dog's judgement of character and followed the man.

We moved back toward the staircase, veering left, and there, just ten feet past, we came upon a wider portion of the tunnel. Set into a brick archway to the right was a transaction window with an iron grill over it, and a hand-painted sign that read 'Teller's Cage'.

"What is this place?" I asked. An arrow on the wall, marked 'Oriental Hotel', pointed further down the corridor. Following its direction beyond the drunken figure urinating against the brick, I spied another doorway, a red lantern burning above, with a steady interchange of patrons.

"Swedish First National Bank," the man replied, leading me around the teller's cage, past a sealed vault, and into a brick alcove behind. "Open day and night for all deposits of Klondike gold. You'll be safe here." He extended a hand as if the place were a luxury suite at the Grand Pacific rather than a dirty recess adorned with cobwebs. I eyed him once or twice, but Sawtooth bid me trust by lying down. I was too tired to fight, too tired to even thank the man. I fell into the corner beside the dog and slept.

When I woke, I was dusted in grey daylight. It fell from glass panels set in the sidewalks above and flickered with the shadows of pedestrians. My eyes were crusted. Every muscle ached, and I suffered a panic that I had fallen asleep and awoken in prison. Sawtooth, though, showed no panic at being confined, his pink tongue curling up at the end in a wide yawn, his great shaggy body stretching. He led me to a bucket of clean water which had not been there the night before and began to lap noisily. In grateful relief, I too drank.

When my benefactor appeared in the thin daylight, I could see his features more clearly, but I had no time to register them, for I had removed most of my clothing to wash away the previous night's filth. Suspicions reawakened, I hid behind Sawtooth, but the stranger was gentlemanly, retreating around the wall. "Pardon me. I only came to tell you my shift is over."

Still unable to conjure the right words for such a situation, I said nothing, quickly pulling my clothing back over my exposed body.

"You should be safe enough during the day," he continued. "I will be back tonight."

"Thank you," I whispered.

"I know you must be hungry. I've left you my lunch pail. I'll bring more food tonight."

Nobody had ever fed me with such kindness, not expecting anything in return, and I was at a loss to understand. "Why are you doing this for me?"

A silence hung in the air for the space of three of my pounding heartbeats, and then he answered. "I'm glad to see you again, Miss Grover Cleveland."

Shame stuck to me like the stinging tendrils of an anemone. I had not asked his name. I had not even recognized him. Perhaps it was his moustache. Or perhaps my own terror. Nevertheless, I felt a peculiar dampness in my soul at the sound of his retreating footfalls.

True to his word, he returned early that night, just before sunset. Sawtooth's wagging homage gave me warning of his approach, and my traitorous heart forgot caution and fluttered in my chest. The man rounded the corner into my alcove with a cheerful "Good evening!" and set a basket beside me. "Some things from my sister Lizzie. For you. I'm sorry they are not new, but I hope they'll fit."

Never having received a gift in my life, I did not know how to behave, but could only finger the soft tissue in awe. When at last the man reached out and folded it open so I might see, I nearly drowned in a rush of feeling. A dress. Clean and pressed, dove grey, with pearl buttons and a neat ruffle at the hem. He was kind enough to look away as I lifted the dress to reveal an assortment of underthings beneath. And shoes. Calfskin. I did not know what to say, only making an alarming croaking noise.

"Oh, do not cry," he said, as I sat down on the wool blanket he had laid on the floor. "I only wanted to thank you."

"Thank me?" I choked. The words sounded foreign to my ear.

He hitched his trousers and sat beside me against the wall. "That day—the day of the fire." He leaned the back of his head against the scarred brick wall. "You saved me."

"I did little. And I didn't even ask your name."

"Edward. Eddie. " His expression misted like steam on glass. "My sister Lizzie and I are alone. Our parents died of tuberculosis on the journey west. That left only me to care for Lizzie."

There was a weight in his voice I knew immediately. Survival was a fraternity. Alone in a boom town with no way to provide, the same threat I faced daily had courted Lizzie as well.

"The very day Lizzie had determined she must accept the poorest of marriage proposals ever offered from the foulest ne'er-do-well, and she only fourteen years old, Mr Smith hired me to clerk in his jewellery store. That was Lizzie's first salvation."

"I had nothing to do with that."

"But then came the fire."

"Surely Mr Smith did not fault you for the fire?"

"He did not. But Smith's shop still burned, and he didn't reopen." Eddie turned grey eyes to me in the dim light. It was a peculiar sensation, unfamiliar and warm in my bones, that those eyes saw not through me nor over me. They saw *me*. "In gratitude for rescuing his inventory," he continued, "Smith gave me a generous gift. A gift that kept us until I found employ with the bank. In fact, a balance remains. But had you not come along that day …" He trailed off, leaving only the growing sounds of licentiousness from down the tunnel and the scurrying of rats.

"I must get to my post." He rose to go. "If you want it, you've a home with us. It's small, but there's room for another."

I do not know where my words came from. They sprouted from the seed of belonging he had offered and pushed into the sunlight. "My name isn't Grover Cleveland."

The chuckle Eddie hid under his expansive moustache was not unkind. "I did suspect as much," he said. "What is your name?"

"I don't know."

He slid back to the floor, bidding me with a raised eyebrow to continue.

"I have no memory from before the old fur trapper. He kept me from very young. Perhaps he came upon me, parents dead from some accident. Perhaps he stole me. Perhaps he is my own father. I do not know." It came out in a frightful rush of tears. But I told him the whole story, reliving it all. My flight from the wilderness. My years of survival in the city. Even the blood on the soles of my shoes.

With such a shameful revelation, surely a man such as Eddie would make a hasty excuse and flee. Instead, his voice was gentle. "Why not just choose a name for yourself?"

"A name is not something you give yourself," I said, brushing the tears away with the back of my hand. Sawtooth laid his head in my lap, and I stroked him. "A name is given to you by someone who cares enough to know you."

My profound statement seemed to find its understanding in silence. With only a nod of acknowledgement, Eddie returned to his work.

The skylights above darkened while I washed with soap, a transcendent experience. Clean, I braided my hair and donned the new dress, utterly changed. While my hands worked, minding their own business, my thoughts were free to wander. Were my senses to be trusted? Might I have a home, or was this nothing more than an elaborate plot for another stranger to take me to his bed?

I lay down on the thick blanket and was wheelbarrowing my thoughts toward sleep when Sawtooth began a low, rumbling growl. Shouts came from every direction, down the tunnels of vice, with assorted thumps on flesh and cries of pain. "Raid," the warnings called out. "Raid!"

I jumped to my feet, but the world tilted under me. As my vision narrowed to only a pinpoint of light, Eddie appeared in the entrance of my alcove. Placing a hand at the back of my neck, he forced my head down until the nausea passed. "It's just a police raid," he murmured. "They'll not bother us. Just stay here."

Gulping deep breaths of air, I shook my head. "No, no, no. They'll want me." I remembered the red light burning far at the end of the corridor. I could still reach it. *Even the police are my clients,* she had said. It wasn't too late. I could be an asset to be protected, fed, and clothed. These thoughts spread like cracks in my courage. Was this to be my punishment for surviving? But as I took one step and then another out of the alcove, Eddie pulled me back. "Trust me," he whispered.

A policeman rapped his club on the bars of the transaction window. He had a face like a headstone, pitted and scarred, and as I stole a peek, I saw him show Eddie a drawing of a girl. "She's about seventeen," he said, his voice like the clanging of rusty fetters. "Wanted for questioning in the suspicious death of Mr Lester Osgood last night. Small, with dark hair. Wears an otter pelt around her neck. Always got a big mutt with her. Nobody knows her name. Maybe ..." He consulted the paper and shrugged. "Adelaide. Josephina. Helga. Have you seen her?"

"No, I have not seen such a girl," Eddie lied.

"Very well, then," the policeman said. "I'll just look around to be sure she's not hiding somewhere."

Backed into the corner of my brick prison, I already felt the policeman's meaty fist closing around my throat. But it was only my otter pelt, slipped aside and pulling at me. Realizing what I wore, I dropped the fur on the floor and bid Sawtooth to come lie on top of it. "Stay," I told my dog. He growled only once and remained firmly anchored, when the policeman discovered our hiding place. The officer's eyes lingered on Sawtooth a beat too long, and then he turned his terrifying scrutiny upon me. "Name," he said.

"She does not speak." Eddie came around to plant himself in front of me, and his voice broke a hole through the veil of my panic. "I speak for her."

The policeman's face darkened. "She looks like the drawing. Right age. A dog. What's her name?"

"Philomena," Eddie said plainly. "Her name is Philomena."

The man's thin-lipped mouth twisted into a sardonic grin. "What kinda half-breed name is that?"

"Philomena, the Princess of Athens, who turned into a hummingbird to escape a lecherous man."

The officer looked dubious. "Last name?"

"Halladay," Eddie answered. "She is my wife." His hand slipped around my waist, fingers resting on my spine. "The dog is ours too. You can tell by the way he behaves that he is no street cur."

The policeman chewed his lip, trying to determine if the Princess of Athens could indeed be a street urchin with no name.

With no chance to test the soundness of the boards before crossing this bridge, a decision propelled me forward in faith. I raised my chin and leaned my body into Eddie's wiry strength. He smelled of woodsmoke and damp wool, and he squeezed me close, even planting a soft kiss on my forehead. I knew nothing of kisses and was surprised at its sweetness.

The police officer's eyes darted about the alcove, taking in the remains of the picnic dinner, the cast-off clothes, the blanket on the floor. At last, with a lascivious grin, he handed the paper to Eddie. "Keep an eye out, then. And a close watch on that pretty wife."

He retreated down the hallway, all the tension following him. I let out my held breath slowly. There remained only one question that seemed important.

"Who would I be to you …" The words caught in my throat, and I looked up at Eddie. "If I came to your home?"

His tone was without guile, and Sawtooth wound around his legs, begging for scratches. "Whoever you want to be," he said, "and nothing you don't."

"Philomena?" I tasted the name, rolling it around in my mouth.

"If you like. It's yours to decide."

"Philomena. It was given to me, and I like it," I said finally, taking his hand. "Philomena."

All living things need names. Mine is Philomena.

THE 2021 MAGPIE AWARD FOR POETRY

THE 2021 MAGPIE AWARD FOR POETRY

In addition to being clever and mischievous, magpies are known for being vocal, and this year's shortlisted Magpies rang loud and true. Our esteemed judge Renée Sarojini Saklikar noted the musicality, rhythm, and attention to sound in each of the winning Magpie poems. Here's what she had to say:

Winner:

'Another True Account of the Nature of Grit and How It May be Ascertained' by Frances Boyle

It's the voice of a strong female lead that won it. Plus: skilled handling of line breaks and stanza construction, ensuring the imaginative narrative flowed easily. I particularly enjoyed the enjambment between stanzas —— the way the lines moved between the poem's paragraphs (stanzas), working on both grammatical and narrative levels. The poem performs as narrative ballad, historical revue, and radio play. What a rattling great read!

First Runner-up:

'Recurrent Dream #79' by David Barrick

Wonderful poem! Reminiscent of poems in John Berryman's fabled Dream Song sequence and Stanley Kunitz's 'The Testing Tree' —— high praise indeed. One stanza, five perfectly balanced sentences constructed over twenty-seven lines. Impeccable grammar and precise line breaks. I loved how the first line neatly frames the question posed in the last line, and the way the title itself embeds the answer. Not to mention the gorgeous imagery.

Second Runner-up:
'Mammal Mouth (*Linaria Vulgaris*)' by Aldona Dziedziejko
A strange poem—one of the highest compliments—filled with fantastical images and interesting line breaks coupled with strong verbs and lush sound.

Honourable Mention:
'Vessel' by Cara Waterfall
Wonderful couplets and a strong rhythmic pulse. This is a poem of delicate grace.

Congratulations to this year's winners and thank you to everyone who submitted to the contest, including our shortlisted authors: David D Barrick, Frances Boyle, Aldona Dziedziejko, Justina Elias, Jude Neale, Pattie Palmer-Baker, Susan C Peters, Cara Waterfall, Claire Wilcox, Trace Wilson.

The winner and runner-up are printed here, and the honourable mention poem will appear in Issue 33, Winter 2022.

__Frances Boyle__ is the author of two books of poetry, most recently This White Nest *(Quattro Books, 2019), along with a short story collection and a novella. Prizes her poetry has won include first place in Arc Poetry Magazine's Diana Brebner contest, and This Magazine's Great Canadian Literary Hunt.* Seeking Shade, *her short story collection, won the Miramichi Reader's Very Best! award for short fiction and was a finalist for both the Danuta Gleed and ReLit awards. Frances's work has been published throughout North America, in the UK and continental Europe, and in India. She lives in Ottawa. Visit francesboyle. com and follow @francesboyle19 on Twitter and Instagram.*

__David Barrick__'s poetry appears in The Fiddlehead, The Malahat Review, Prairie Fire, EVENT, *and other literary journals. He is Managing Director of the Antler River Poetry (formerly Poetry London) reading series (Ontario)* and author of the chapbook Incubation Chamber. *His full-length collection,* Nightlight, *will be published by Palimpsest Press in spring 2022.*

Aldona Dziedziejko *is a first-generation immigrant writer and educator. Her poetry and creative nonfiction have appeared in CV2, subTerrain, Poetry is Dead, BAD Dog Review, The Ekphrastic Review, Northern Appeal, Humble Pie, Sky Island Journal, The Capilano Review, Fiction Southeast, and elsewhere. She has also received the Lina Chartrand Poetry Award (CV2). These days, she's working on a poetry manuscript, Clickbait, that explores the technology/nature dichotomy and human origins. She is a settler and teacher in a Northern Canadian hamlet in the Tlicho region belonging to the Dene people.*

Another True Account of the Nature of Grit and How It May Be Ascertained

by Frances Boyle

The world and heaven itself bring me back to this story
writ in my hand with plain-spoken probity, and I hope
a certain humility. My name is Mattie Ross, and I speak,
to take a leaf from my own book, of the time when I,
only fourteen years of age, set off for Choctaw Nation
in the snow, bound to avenge the blood of my father,
shot by Tom Chaney. I called him coward and trash,
and no truer words were ever told of a man.

When I had departed from earth, Mr Charles Portis
took up what I had written, published it as his own. *True
Grit* he called that book. God-fearing, woman and girl,
I watched from this celestial vantage place, not
so very much lovelier after all than Mount Magazine
in the Blue Mountains near my home, highest point

in the whole of Arkansas. I felt no shame to have,
after so much time, my journey laid out for viewing.

A tale kept under wraps becomes, as they say, etiolated,
a scrawny twisted stem, pinworm white, you might find
beneath a thick piece of dogwood bark fallen
where new bean plants struggle to break earth. No,
for bringing my story to the light, I would surely
have welcomed Mr Charles Portis any time to my table
with the kindest courtesy I could conjure. But, sorrow
to say, I have few good words for the moving-picture show

that called itself *True Grit*, and one Mr John Wayne
play-acting US Marshal Cogburn, known as Rooster.
Mr Cogburn had been christened Reuben, a fine name
regretfully I ascertained only as I paid for each letter
inscribed on his headstone, along with dates to mark
his birth and his death. I say now, as I have said before,
despite the thirst he would too often slake, and his penchant
for taking the Lord's name in vain, Reuben Cogburn had grit.

Mr Wayne, who tells me his name at birth was Marion,
is a good man though his flicker-form had not the true aspect
of Marshall Cogburn. But I heard tell just the other day (year?
news comes slow here sometimes) that another photoplay
of my quest for justice is being crafted, its makers two brothers,
not Christians by their family name, but well thought of.
I will hold but faint hope that the grit that spurred us through
dire exploits will show in the miens of their new players.

But know that the recounting of how I rode with lawmen
to avenge my father is not the story of Reuben Cogburn,
but of me, Mattie Ross, Yell County, Arkansas.
I do not boast of my gifts or learning, and even less
of my features and face, by all accounts plain indeed.
The girl in that first film-show was a pretty little thing.
The snake bite did not take her arm, as it did mine,
leaving me to live by wits, my piety and my resolve.

Recurrent Dream #79

by David Barrick

At my birthday party,
I play hide and seek
in the Muskoka woods.
Ollie ollie oxen free
I call, bears and badgers
ducking under bushes,
toadstools shriveling
back into logs. I search
burrows using a sparkler,
but as dusk arrives, I've
only found my own face:
the yellowing lost child poster
on lichen-covered trunks.
You've gone too deep
whisper lines of patio lanterns,
angling my eyes across
the lake to stiff bodies
left in slatted beach chairs.

A Mark Hamill mask dangles
on a camping lamp, ogling foliage
with wind-cajoled eyebeams.
The walnuts and pinecones
and acorns wrapped with foil
paper—red fireworks inside
the forest's thistle womb,
fledgling nightingales singing:
how old are you now?

Mammal Mouth (Linaria Vulgaris)

by Aldona Dziedziejko

If God didn't
want us to kiss
animal mouths
why make them so exquisite—
vibrissae,
whiskered velvet purses.
Don't get me
wrong, I don't believe in God
as sentient architect
like that. But
the logic speaks
for itself here. It whispers, huffs
brushing its breath
against bacteria,
innervated fur,
pink-ham tongue. Saliva.

Look—here
is another mouth, a waxy rind
lobed, glossed,
head held low, slow woolly hedge
sliding past our railing.

Dogs steal scraps fallen under the house.
The Full Worm Moon this March makes me
think of slithering. Burying pupae in crumbling, warm soil.

How we still fear virions twisting
in their envelopes.
I call them *diamondheads*,
like sugar crystals poured
into our bodies,
frothing, fomenting, seething in havoc.

I hope that in the days of the sun
toadflax turn their faces up,
yellow cheeks full of air.
Our future is
hungry, like a Snapdragon, a growing
Lion's Mouth or Dead
Man's Bones
taking root in lime soil,
somatosensory—
it wants to take what you are made to give.

Here in the North, we kiss
river mouths for good luck, ponds

gobble up arsenic, spit
out heart shaped leaves,
like green muzzles
and the groundwater makes superheroes
of the dying.

HOUSES

Matthew Nielsen

Matthew Nielsen, also known by the pen name Nuclear Jackal, is currently working on Toni and Aberdeen, a comic about time travellers living in an empty 2003 Vancouver. In this issue we bring you part two of 'Houses', a graphic story inspired by the many moves in Matthew's own life. He now lives in Canada, and as of this writing has just moved house again. In the meantime, he uploads his illustrations to Instagram @nuclearjackal. Part one of 'Houses' appears in Issue 31, Summer 2021.

BY MATTHEW NIELSEN
HOUSES
A COMIC ABOUT THE 11 OR SO PLACES I'VE LIVED IN

UNIVERSITY WAS IN HEREFORD. SO INSTEAD OF DOING A DAILY TWO-HOUR COMMUTE VIA THE UNRELIABLE NATIONAL RAIL, I LIVED IN A STUDIO APARTMENT IN A TERRACED HOUSE DURING THE TERM.
IT COST ABOUT THE SAME IN RENT AS THE TICKETS WOULD HAVE ANYHOW.
2ND STOREY
IT WAS A COZY, LONELY APARTMENT.
WITH LOUD NEIGHBOURS OCCASIONALLY, BUT NOT CONSTANTLY.
INITIALLY ALL I HAD FOR INTERNET ACCESS WAS AN EXPENSIVE PAY-AS-YOU-GO MOBILE DATA USB ADAPTER FOR MY LAPTOP.
250 MB FOR £5 GBP ($10 CAD ABOUT AT THE TIME)
BECAUSE YOUTUBE VIDEOS WERE TOO EXPENSIVE WITH THIS PLAN, I INSTEAD BOUGHT ABOUT A HUNDRED VHS TAPES FOR 10 PENCE APIECE AND WATCHED THEM ON MY VCR.
ALSO, I READ SHEDLOADS OF GRAPHIC NOVELS.

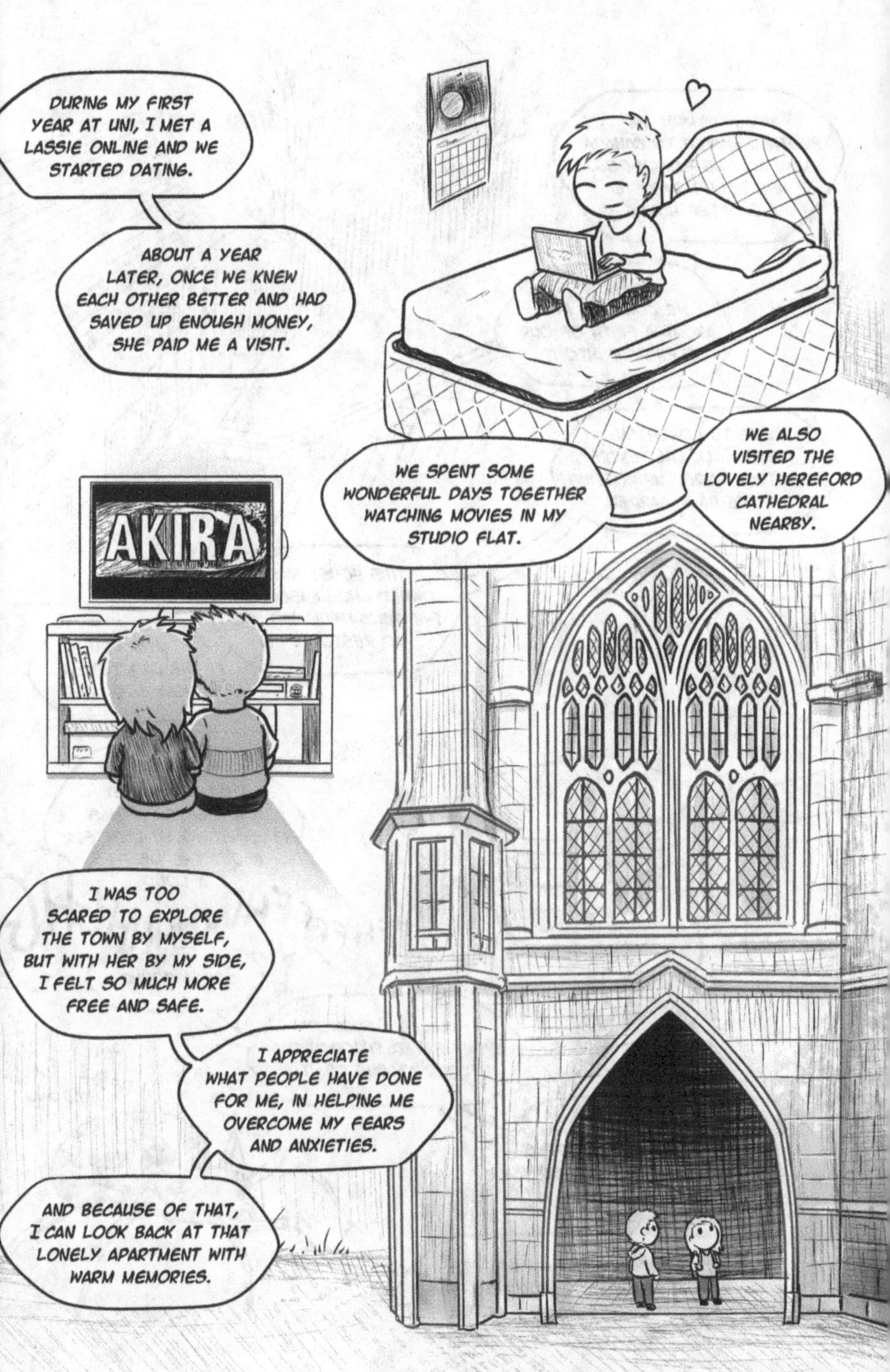

DURING MY FIRST YEAR AT UNI, I MET A LASSIE ONLINE AND WE STARTED DATING.
ABOUT A YEAR LATER, ONCE WE KNEW EACH OTHER BETTER AND HAD SAVED UP ENOUGH MONEY, SHE PAID ME A VISIT.
WE SPENT SOME WONDERFUL DAYS TOGETHER WATCHING MOVIES IN MY STUDIO FLAT.
WE ALSO VISITED THE LOVELY HEREFORD CATHEDRAL NEARBY.
AKIRA
I WAS TOO SCARED TO EXPLORE THE TOWN BY MYSELF, BUT WITH HER BY MY SIDE, I FELT SO MUCH MORE FREE AND SAFE.
I APPRECIATE WHAT PEOPLE HAVE DONE FOR ME, IN HELPING ME OVERCOME MY FEARS AND ANXIETIES.
AND BECAUSE OF THAT, I CAN LOOK BACK AT THAT LONELY APARTMENT WITH WARM MEMORIES.

WHEN MY MUM AND BROTHER MOVED TO CANADA, MY DAD, THE FAMILY DOG, AND I ALL MOVED TO A SMALLER HOUSE.
IN FACT, WE COULDN'T FIT ABOUT A FIFTH OF OUR FURNITURE INTO IT.
DUE TO LOGISTICAL ISSUES, ALL THAT EXTRA FURNITURE ENDED UP ROTTING IN THE BACK GARDEN.
THIS HOUSE WAS OWNED AND LEASED BY THE DELIGHTFUL MAN WHO HAD RESTORED IT.
MIND YOU, HE DIDN'T DO A VERY GOOD JOB.
THE NOISE THAT THE TOILET MADE AFTER IT WAS FLUSHED WOULD LAST FOR ABOUT TWO MINUTES. A LOUD
FFFFHFHFFFFHWHHHHGHG
SORTA SOUND.
HELL, THE SHOWER EVEN LEAKED THROUGH THE FLOOR AT ONE POINT.
THE HOUSE WAS ORIGINALLY BUILT USING COAL DUST, AND WE LIVED NEAR A MOTORWAY, SO I WAS OFTEN COUGHING.
IT WAS SO DAMP THAT SPIDERS WERE EVERYWHERE. I STOPPED BEING SCARED OF THEM IN THIS HOUSE.
THE NOBLE FALSE WIDOW

AROUND THIS TIME, DAD HAD BEEN EXPERIENCING A COLD FOR A LONG WHILE. LIKE A YEAR OR SO.
HE HAD GONE TO THE DOCTORS MANY TIMES, BUT WAS ALWAYS TOLD IT WOULD BLOW OVER.
WELL IT TURNED OUT TO BE HENOCH-SCHÖNLEIN PURPURA AND IGA NEPHROPATHY; A DEADLY SORT OF VASCULITIS.
HE GOT SKIN LESIONS ALL OVER HIS BODY, AND NEARLY DIED.
I THINK HE HAD A ONE IN FOUR CHANCE OF DEATH, BUT VERY FORTUNATELY HE SURVIVED.
FOR A LONG TIME HE HAD NO IMMUNE SYSTEM, AND NO SENSE OF TASTE.
AND HE GOT A MILD STROKE ON TOP OF ALL THAT.
DURING HIS RECOVERY, HE WALKED THE FAMILY DOG EACH DAY.
EVENTUALLY I FINISHED UNIVERSITY, SKIPPED THE GRADUATION CEREMONY, AND ME, MY DOG, AND MY DAD ALL MOVED TO CANADA.
WE LOADED EVERYTHING INTO A SHIPPING CONTAINER, AND TOOK A PLANE TO CANADA.

DURING THE TRIP, A MANCHESTERIAN WOMAN DECIDED TO BECOME OUR FRIEND.
WE WERE OKAY WITH IT UNTIL WE FOUND OUT SHE WAS RACIST.
YACKITY SMACKITY BLAH BLAH BLAH!
I WANTED TO TELL HER TO SHOVE OFF, BUT MY DAD WOULDN'T LET ME.
MY MUM, SISTERS, AND BROTHER MET US AT THE AIRPORT, AND OUR DOG TOOK A DRINK FROM THE FOUNTAIN OUTSIDE THE AIRPORT.
MY AUNT LET US STAY AT HER HOUSE FOR A MONTH WHILST WE WAITED FOR THE SHIPPING CONTAINER TO ARRIVE.
HERE I GOT MY FIRST TOUCH-SCREEN SMARTPHONE (LATE TO THE PARTY).
WITHIN A FEW HOURS, I HAD ACCIDENTALLY SENT IT THROUGH THE WASH.
CANADA IS ABOUT AS CLOSE TO THE UK AS YOU CAN GET, ASIDE FROM AUS AND NZ I GUESS.
STILL, IT WAS ALL SO DIFFERENT FOR ME. THE STREETS WERE WIDER, TREES WERE TALLER, AND THE PRODUCE WAS BIGGER.

MUM AND DAD SOON FOUND US A HOUSE GOING AT AN AFFORDABLE PRICE.
WHAT MADE IT SO CHEAP WAS THAT IT WAS DUE TO BE TORN DOWN IN A YEAR OR TWO TO MAKE WAY FOR A BIGGER BUILDING.

THE OWNERS WHOM WE RENTED IT FROM HAD BOUGHT IT FROM AN OLD MAN.
MY DAD RECKONED THAT THE OLD MAN'S WIFE HAD PASSED AWAY, SO HIS CHILDREN CONVINCED HIM TO SELL THE HOUSE AND MOVE TO A CARE HOME.
THE PROBLEM WAS, THE OLD MAN CAME OVER A COUPLE OF TIMES, LETTING HIMSELF INTO THE BACK YARD, IN ORDER TO GIVE US ADVICE.

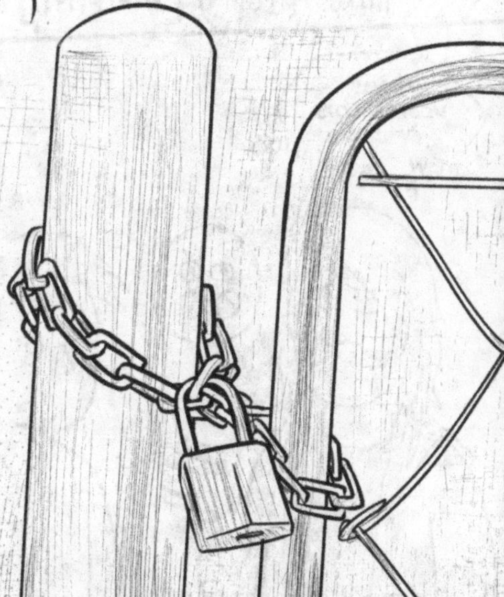

SO MY DAD PUT A CHAIN ON THE GATE. ONE TIME THE OLD MAN TRIED TO GET IN, BUT THE DOG BARKED, AND HE NEVER CAME BACK.
HE PROBABLY REGRETTED SELLING THE HOUSE IN THE FIRST PLACE.

WHEN THE FREIGHT CONTAINER ARRIVED, MY SISTERS ASKED SOME FRIENDS FOR HELP.
THEIR HELP WAS FANTASTIC, AND WE GOT EVERYTHING SHIFTED IN RECORD TIME.
I FEEL A BIT ASHAMED TO ADMIT IT, BUT SEEING AS I WAS STILL QUITE BEHIND ON MY SOCIAL SKILLS, IT WAS ONLY THEN THAT I GOT MY FIRST EVER REGULAR JOB.
I BEGAN WORKING AT A SUPERMARKET AS A GENERAL CLERK.
SO THINGS GOT A WHOLE LOT MORE STRESSFUL FOR ME DURING THIS TIME.
BERK
YOU PEOPLE NEVER GET THESE THINGS RIGHT.
YES MA'AM.
I WAS MEETING LOTS OF JERKS NEW AQUAINTANCES
I STILL HAD A LOT OF GROWING UP TO DO, WHETHER I LIKED IT OR NOT.
BATHROO
AND BEFORE I KNEW IT, WE WERE MOVING AGAIN.

THE HOUSE WE WERE IN WAS FINALLY SCHEDULED FOR DEMOLITION, SO WE MOVED ON TO ANOTHER ONE.
THIS ONE WAS SPLIT BETWEEN TWO FAMILIES. OURS UPSTAIRS, AND ANOTHER DOWNSTAIRS.
THE ONLY SHARED FACILITY WAS THE LAUNDRY ROOM. OTHER THAN THAT, WE DIDN'T HAVE TO INTERACT.
STILL, THAT FAMILY WAS A PAIN IN THE ARSE.
PLAYING LOUD MUSIC IN THEIR GARDEN WELL PAST MIDNIGHT.
AND CAUSING THE MOUSE INFESTATION.
USING UP 75% OF THE ELECTRICITY BILL AND TRYING TO GET US TO GO 50/50 ON IT.
(GOOD THING WE GOT A METER INSTALLED)
WE LIVED NEAR A LANDFILL, SO THE AIR USUALLY STANK.
I KINDA GET NOSTALGIA FROM THAT SMELL WHENEVER I PASS THAT AREA.

I GOT FIRED FROM MY FIRST JOB: FAIR ENOUGH.
SO I STARTED WORKING NIGHT SHIFTS INSTEAD, THIS TIME AT A DIFFERENT SUPERMARKET.
FECK OFF!
FECK ON!
Shop 4 food
40%!!
FOODWAY
THOSE WERE ROTTEN TIMES.
I WAS GLAD THAT I DIDN'T HAVE TO DEAL WITH CUSTOMER SERVICE ANYMORE, BUT I BEGAN FILLING UP WITH DOUBT AND HATE.
I ENTERED SOME SORT OF DEPRESSION. IT TOOK A LONG TIME TO CLIMB OUT OF THAT HOLE.
EVENTUALLY I GOT SO FED UP THAT I LEFT THE JOB. I TOOK A THREE MONTH TRIP TO FINLAND TO VISIT MY GIRLFRIEND.
IT COST ALL I HAD SAVED UP, BUT THAT WAS A MAGICAL SUMMER.
DELICIOUS RYE BREAD!
U-TOW
AND THE GREAT NEWS WAS THAT THE FAMILY HAD MOVED AGAIN WHILST I WAS AWAY.

SO I CAME BACK TO A NEW HOUSE.

SAME DEAL AS THE HOUSE BEFORE. IT'S OURS TILL IT GETS DEMOLISHED.

A BETTER NEIGHBOURHOOD, CRAP INSULATION, AND LOTS OF SPACE.

THERE'S A HALF-DEAD CHERRY TREE IN OUR GARDEN

OUR WELSH DOG MET A SKUNK FOR THE FIRST TIME.

FRIEND?

!!

AND SMELLED OF BURNT TIRES AND WEED UNTIL THE END OF HIS DAYS.

THE HOUSE WAS QUITE POPULATED. FOR A LONG TIME THERE WAS:

MY MUM & DAD,

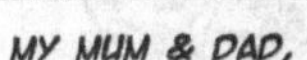

MY ELDEST SISTER,

HER HUSBAND,

THEIR TWO CHILDREN,

MY OTHER SISTER,

MY BROTHER,

PLUS ME AND THE DOG AND ALL THAT.

WE ENDED UP WITH A BUNCH OF RABBITS LIVING IN OUR GARDEN.
IT WAS QUITE AN ENJOYABLE SIGHT TO WAKE UP TO EACH DAY.
AFTER MY SISTERS MOVED OUT, MY GIRLFRIEND CAME TO STAY FOR A BIT.
AND I'VE GOTTA SAY, IT'S NICE TO FINALLY BE ABLE TO LIVE TOGETHER AFTER ABOUT EIGHT YEARS OF LONG DISTANCING.
SURE IT'S DAMP, COLD, AND SOMETHING BREAKS EVERY FIVE MINUTES,
BUT THIS IS THE HAPPIEST I'VE BEEN IN A LONG TIME.
PLOP!
AND I RECENTLY FOUND OUT THAT THERE'S A GOOD CHANCE THE FAMILY WILL BE MOVING ONCE AGAIN SOON.
NOT SURE HOW I FEEL ABOUT THAT.

SO THAT'S THE STORY THUS FAR.
I COULD HAVE EXPANDED EACH OF THESE LITTLE BITS AND BOBS TO A FEW PAGES EACH. AND THERE ARE LOADS MORE STORIES TO TELL.
AND THAT'S JUST ABOUT HOUSES. I STILL WANT TO SHARE MY EXPERIENCES WITH AUTISM AND THE EDUCATION SYSTEM,
OR SOME OF THE PEOPLE I MET DURING MY TIME AS A SHOE SHINER.
AND THE THINGS MY PARENTS DID WHILE THEY WERE GROWING UP.
HOUSES
I KNOW I COMPLAIN ABOUT A GOOD CHUNK OF THINGS, BUT PLENTY OF FOLK HAD IT TOUGHER THAN ME.
MARJANE SATRAPI'S NEIGHBOURHOOD GOT HIT BY MISSLE STRIKES.
BILL GUARNERE AND BABE HEFRON GREW UP DURING THE GREAT DEPRESSION.
LENNY HENRY EXPERIENCED RACISM AND BETRAYAL FROM HIS BEST FRIEND.
AIRBORNE
READING ABOUT THOSE EXPERIENCES MAKES ME APPRECIATE THE LUCK I'VE HAD IN MY LIFE.
AND I HOPE YOU CONSIDER SHARING SOME STORIES TOO, IF YOU LIKE.
DRAWINGS MAKE IT MORE FUN FOR ME TO READ 'EM AND WRITE 'EM.

THE SHEPHERDESS: INTRIGUE

JM Landels

Toinette has moved up in the world, from shepherdess to maid to the pretend sister of the Chevalier de Foix, but her mistress, the Countess, has been laid low by poison. While the Countess recovers, Toinette must negotiate the complexities of the court at Versailles in her guise as the daughter of a noble family.

JM Landels *is torn between travelling the world to teach writing and swordfighting, and never leaving her idyllic farm in Langley, BC. Her debut series, fantasy bestseller* Allaigna's Song: Overture, *and the sequel,* Aria, *are available from Pulp Literature Press and Amazon. You can follow her adventures with pen and sword at jmlandels.stiffbunnies.com.*

The Shepherdess: Intrigue

The Queen was a tiny woman, whose feet rested on a gilded footstool beneath the stiff skirts of her old-fashioned Spanish-style dress. With a miniscule silver fork, she plucked a morsel from the bowl of coquilles Saint Jacques at her side and slipped it between fleshy lips. She put down the fork with deliberate care and at last motioned me forward.

I approached, curtseyed, and willed my stomach not to revolt at the smell of the seafood. The ground oyster shell that Madame had dusted over my face tickled my nose, and the cochineal on my lips doubled my inclination to sneeze. I bit my lip to stop the sneeze, and the taste of rouge nearly made me vomit instead.

Michel had already made the introduction, so there was nothing I needed to say as the little Queen appraised me. She addressed her questions to him.

"Is she skilled with the needle?" She pronounced it *a-gual* with her Spanish accent, so I barely understood her.

Michel cleared his throat. "I believe the sisters valued her work in the garden above all."

She eyed me again. "Odd work for the daughter of a noble family."

I responded before Michel could dig me further into a hole out of which I would not be able to clamber.

"The herb and flower gardens, Your Majesty," I said, mimicking Michel's accent as best I could. "I … made creams and healing salves." I could at least make a balm for a ewe with a sore udder. "Powders and colours for the faces and hands of noble ladies." Another partial truth. But how hard could it be to grind up seashells and add pigments to my lanolin mixtures?

She sniffed. "A young lady should be taught to sew, to sing, and to dance."

"Indeed, Your Majesty," interjected Michel. "Which is why, with the passing of our beloved parents and her education falling to me, I have brought her here for the improvement of her mind and soul."

Marie-Therese extended a be-ringed hand. "I shall contemplate it, Chevalier."

I took the childlike fingers and kissed the air above them as Michel had instructed, noticing the redness of the knuckles and the chafing where the rings bit into flesh. I could fix that, I thought, given the chance.

After we had left Her Majesty, Michel remarked, "That did not go as badly as it might have."

"She seemed unimpressed."

He shrugged. "Her Majesty is unimpressed with life. 'Contemplate' rather than a simple 'no' is a good sign. Now, we return to your apartments so you can refresh your toilette. The Duchesse d'Orleans is next."

The King's sister-in-law was even more difficult to parse. German was her first language, and her speech was animated, unlike the careful sentences of the Queen. Also unlike the Queen, she showed a keen interest in my professed skills.

"My dear, your skin is as fresh as a shepherdess's," she exclaimed, leaning toward me with a pair of spectacles on a long stick. "And no cracks. How do you compound your ceruse?"

"Madame," I replied, "I never use ceruse," which was truthful enough. "It dulls the skin and deadens the senses. Instead, a cream made of"—I hesitated, realizing where my worth lay—"rare, nourishing ingredients, dusted over with a special powder …" No need to tell her she could attain it from the kitchen waste. I had momentum now, and my tongue got ahead of me. "… As well as tonics taken internally, will give your skin the pastoral glow you crave." That part was not true at all—spend time in pastures, and your skin will turn brown as a walnut. Which was why I no longer did.

"*Wunderbar!*" exclaimed the Duchess. "You shall bring me these tomorrow. Enough for Philippe as well. He wears far too much makeup, and his skin is a wreck."

"Madame," I stammered, "I will happily bring you what I can, but my supplies are low." I took a deep breath. "A week, to brew tonic and make fresh creams."

She made a mock pout. "Well, then. I shall be patient. We will be great friends, you and I, I think."

I held my breath as I left. A week, I had, to invent a tonic and extricate myself from this new trap I'd walked into.

I did not have the social standing to send for the surgeon—I had to call on him instead. That was just a well, for I suspected that what I wanted I would find at his location. Convincing Michel Dubois to take me there was another challenge altogether.

His pale eyebrows shot up, making his innocent face look younger than ever. "Send a messenger, why don't you? Surely there is no need to leave the palace gates on an errand? And if it is women's needs that concern you, there are a number of discreet ladies within the palace to call upon. Even if it is," he dropped his voice, "an abortion you require."

"M'sieur!" I exclaimed. Only the fact I was not as far up the social ladder as I one day intended to be prevented me from slapping him. "It is nothing of the sort. I merely require a reliable source of flowers and herbs."

He shrugged. "There are far more flowers within the palace gardens than without. But if you are so determined, who am I to hinder you? Fortunately, it is lovely weather for a stroll."

Thus it was I found myself walking at a courtly pace—not my usual rolling stride—through the broad avenues of the town. The old hameau had been almost entirely obliterated by the gilt and glass palace, Michel explained, and uniform and orderly houses had replaced the ancient cottages on meandering cow paths that comprised most villages.

It was a relief to walk among ordinary people again: street vendors with baskets upon their heads, swineherds driving their pigs to market, tinkers and knife grinders with their tools set up on the street corner. Even night soil carts were a welcome sight after the mannered artifice of the court. I released my grip on Michel's arm and let my hips swing as I walked, relaxing into as long a stride as my pattens would allow.

We knocked—not just scratched—upon the blue-painted door of No 5 rue de la Paroisse. We were greeted by the housekeeper. "Have you an appointment?" she asked.

Michel swept the ground with the plume of his hat. "We do not. Please tell Dr Ahmed that the Chevalier de Foix and his sister await his earliest convenience."

The doctor's earliest convenience turned out to be more than half an hour out, but I entertained myself while waiting by casting my eye about the fascinating contents of the surgeon's drawing room. Aside from the macabre human skeleton, which was missing a leg, there were bottles of tripe in red liquid, a stuffed cat, and a brightly coloured bird I didn't recognize. Michel passed his time by trimming his nails with a small knife.

At last the door opened and the surgeon appeared, wiping his hands on a stained butcher's apron.

"Mademoiselle," he said, surprised. "I hope your mistress hasn't taken a turn for the worse?"

"Indeed no," I said. "I've come to take you up on your offer."

"My offer?"

"Of apprenticing as a pharmacist," I said, barely daring to breathe. "I believe we have much to offer each other. You have herbs, flowers and the means to manufacture medicines for improving beauty and health, while I"—I had to pause to inhale at last—"have commissions from both the Duchess d'Orleans and the Queen herself."

And so began one of my busiest but happiest times at Versailles. Thrice weekly I would walk to Dr Ahmed's home in rue de la Paroisse, dressed in my maid's clothes and eschewing Michel's escort. There, I would grind substances in the mortars, infuse them in glass carafes, or chafe them in the alembic, releasing and transforming their properties while Dr Ahmed read to me in Latin, Greek, and Arabic. Though I knew little of these tongues, save from the priest's Latin that I tended to sleep through, he always paused to translate the meaningful words into the other two languages and French, giving me a passing familiarity with each.

The Queen and the Duchess were each pleased in their own way with the skin creams I produced: the former with a stiff nod and a softening of her cold, watery eyes, the latter with effusive hugs and kisses that defied the notion of Austrians as a reserved people. Liselotte, as the Duchess now insisted I call her, began teaching me to read in French and German, so I developed an eye for these languages as they lived on paper.

As the pretend sister of Michel Dubois, I had access to parts of the court I would not have as Madame's maid-in-waiting. But the greater scrutiny I received felt perilous. To hide my country accent, I spoke as little as possible but listened much, repeating the clipped aristocratic words inside my closed mouth. In the appartement, I practised out loud in the looking glass, shaping my lips and tilting my head in the manner of the ladies I observed. It was all in the way of holding oneself, I began to feel. Disguise was a matter of mimicry and bearing more than physical appearance.

Early on, when Madame was still recovering from her poisoning, I posed in front of the mirror and tested my fan, the angle of my feet, and my coquettish laugh. I heard a cough from behind me. Madame leaned on the doorframe, wrapped in the counterpane from her bed, looking more like a washerwoman than a Countess.

"Madame." I threw down my fan and rushed to her side. "Should you be up?"

"Well, Toinette, I called and waited — but never mind. I think it's better that I begin to move myself."

"Let me at least help you into a morning robe," I said.

"Yes, that would be nice," she agreed. "And then a pot of tisane, I think."

"I wasn't born a countess, you know," she said as I poured her a cup of rose-petal tea. "Some for yourself too, Toinette. And sit. Now that we have trained you so well as a handmaiden, you must break those habits and become a lady."

I obeyed, perching on the edge of the armless chair, for my panniers didn't allow me to sit full on it.

She extended a blue-veined hand and gazed at it. "I was born with this white skin, but when I was young it was as brown as Henri's."

I felt that must be an exaggeration, and said so. She cocked an eyebrow. "Not Moorish, no," she admitted. "And not as smooth and ripe as yours was, my Romany girl, when you first arrived fresh off the field. I was splotched and freckled like a red cow. I herded cattle and milked them, planted corn, killed chickens, and rode an ass to market on Saturdays. Until one day the young laird rode by, well in his cups after the hunt, and spied me pulling beetroots."

She paused, sipped her tea, and closed her eyes. I could see that sitting upright was taking a toll on her. To help her along, I concluded the story for her. "He fell in love, and in time made you his countess?"

Her green eyes opened. "He raped me, there in the field, and left me covered in mud, blood, and the red stains of beet greens."

My teacup rattled as I dropped it the last half inch into its saucer. I put it down with shaking hands. She held hers out, and I refilled it.

At last I asked. "Did he leave you with child, regret his actions, and then ..."

"Make me a countess? No, love. No one made me a countess." There was another long pause. "At least I was not with child," she continued. "No, I bade farewell to my father and mother and went to the castle in search of employment. I worked as a scullery maid, and then a serving maid, and then a cook. You see, it was my intent to poison him." She looked at me with those glass-green eyes, seeing if I would register shock, perhaps.

I poured myself a second cup of tea. "Did you?"

"I didn't need to. He fell off his horse and broke his neck in a ditch. So there I was, in position to exact revenge—and with no one to exact it upon, you might think. But there was. His drunken wretch of a father, who lay his fat hands on every servant girl who got within range, or his two brothers, the one who took maids by command and the other who took them with pretty words. None was better than the others. I was never raped again, but I suffered my share of groping and wine-soaked busses. Poisoning them all would leave me, and all the other servants like me, with no employment. So instead I stole clothes, coins, and jewels from the lady of the castle, and a horse from the stable. I fled to Dublin, and from there took ship to Blackpool. I sold some jewels, and travelled by coach to Kingston and by ship to Rotterdam. I picked up a maidservant along the way, and then a footman. By the time I reached Paris, I was the Countess of Athlone, fallen on hard times, fleeing Holland for the safety of a Catholic country. Mathilde was my maidservant, Henri my valet. So you see, my dear, we are not so different, you and I."

A cowherd and a shepherd, posing as courtiers under the nose of the King of France, I mused as I emptied the dregs of the teapot into the swill bucket. Was anyone here what they purported to be?

A month or two later, when Madame had recovered and begun travelling to and from court without us for reasons of her own, Marie-Claire and I had settled into a knotty relationship as co-workers who occasionally served as the other's maidservant.

"Where did this ribband come from?" asked Claire as she tied it into my hair, her hint of a frown barely visible in the glass.

I thought at first to lie, to say it was from Liselotte, but I couldn't resist the flutter of warmth when I let slip, "Antoine de Barreau."

Her fingers froze for the barest instant, then continued with my hair, perhaps less gently than before. My supposed relation to Michel Dubois had opened doors for me within the court that were closed to her. "I am going to the village tomorrow," I said. "Company on the walk would be nice."

She put away the curling tongs and brushes with a clatter. "Is this your idea of charity? I could walk to the village on my own if I chose. And why would I want to visit that foul-smelling apothecary?"

Fasoul's workshop was redolent with strange odours, but foul was not the adjective I would have chosen. Marie-Claire's nose was as keen as mine, but differently tuned.

I cleared my throat. "I'm not going to Dr Ahmed's. It is a promenade, with Michel, Daphné, and her cousin Antoine."

She stood looking at me, her hands on her hips, that peculiar frown balanced between her thin pale eyebrows. "Peut-être," she said, "but you will have to do my hair."

Michel was unfazed when I showed up the next morning with Claire. He kissed her on the fingers and me on each cheek as a friend and a brother should. Daphné was less insouciant, as this disrupted her carefully planned outing, which would have paired me with her cousin so she could take Michel's arm.

Antoine was delighted, though. "One for each arm!" he exclaimed, linking his left elbow through Claire's and offering me his right.

Michel and Daphné walked ahead of us, deep in animated conversation as we strolled past the ornate black-and-gilt carriage gates and onto the cobbled road.

Daphné's cousin kept a stream of words going — the weather, the gardens, Claire's golden curls and my dark ones, the fine gaits of the carriage horses that clopped past us — but, try as I might, I could not find an interesting word to return. My mind drifted away under the drone of his talk and Claire's appreciative murmurs and *oui, monsieur*s. I let myself enjoy the feeling of a man's arm through my own while my eye focussed on the black ringlets under Daphne's wide hat, which bobbed in time with the ostrich plume on Michel's.

We stopped beneath the shade of a plane tree. Michel went into the nearby tavern to fetch glasses of pression while Antoine stood, one foot on the edge of a horse trough, and regaled us with a tale of some courtier's lost slipper, which I followed not at all. His calf, clad in pale silk, was longer than Michel's though not so finely muscled, but it was pleasing to the eye nonetheless. Suddenly I could stand the dull buzz of conversation no longer. "My pardon." I rose from the bench, curtseying. "I have just remembered an errand."

Making my excuses to my puzzled companions, I hurried off to Dr Ahmed's place on rue de la Paroisse.

"Mon dieu," I said to Fasoul. "I do not think I could endure another minute of such tedious conversation."

Dr Ahmed looked at me over the rim of the alembic, into which he was titrating a solution of slaked lye. "And your sheep were better conversationalists, back when you lived in St Geneviève?" he asked.

"A sheep can be trusted not to open its mouth except to convey some important information, such as 'I'm lost, I'm stuck, I'm hungry'."

His curly grey eyebrows lifted, though he didn't stop his titration. "And what information do your fashionable young friends convey?"

"What the King said about the grouse at dinner last night. What the Marquise de Montespan is wearing. How Mademoiselle de Fontanges is piling her curls upon her head rather than over her ears. The bleating of sheep is far more interesting."

"Ah, but would I, who knew a passing number of horses and camels in my time but never a sheep, be able to understand which bleats were hunger and which were sorrow?"

"Likely not."

"And can you, who have not suckled upon the teat of the court, interpret your companion's bleatings? The young man who commented on the King's opinion of fowl was in truth reminding you all that he sits close enough to His Majesty to be part of the conversation. The demoiselle who remarks upon the flowing gowns Madame de Montespan uses to disguise her growing girth is inviting comparison to her own slender appearance. And she who informed you of the hairstyle of the Fontanges woman was offering a valuable hint about who is rising and falling at court—implying, perhaps, that she is knowledgeable of such."

I blinked, astonished at Fasoul's insightful assessment.

"The content of small talk is nothing," he continued. "The context is everything."

"But how do *you* understand this language?" I asked. I could hardly see Dr Ahmed taking part in the idle chatter of the court.

"I speak half a dozen languages and read as many more again. This is one you should add to your studies. At least it shares the same words as your native tongue."

"But how?" I asked. "When you teach me Latin and Greek, you compare it to French. I have no guide when I am in society."

"The Countess?"

"Is so often away from court lately that I barely see her."

"That is a pity," said Fasoul. "The Chevalier de Foix would be your next best interpreter, but——" He stopped himself, peering at me again. "No. That won't do."

"The Duchess d'Orleans …" he posited.

"Believes me to be the Chevalier's sister. I can't expose my ignorance to her."

"Very well, you must make an independent study, but I will help you. You will make note of conversation—not just what courtiers say, but what they do, where they stand, who they look at, and when they turn their backs or cast their eyes down."

I opened my mouth to protest, but the doctor lifted a finger. "Your handwriting is abysmal—you could use the extra practice. Bring these reports to me and interpret them. Start by recounting today."

When I closed Fasoul's blue-painted door behind me, the shadows of the buildings opposite nearly touched my feet. I tied my mask back on nonetheless, for the shadows would not protect my complexion once I passed into the sunny palace grounds. How easily offended my skin was, I reflected, now that I no longer spent my days in the pastures.

My peripheral vision thus impaired, I failed to notice Michel Dubois until he fell into step beside me, elbow extended.

"You startled me, m'sieur," I said, taking his arm reluctantly. "Have you been waiting all this time?"

"Bien sûr. You didn't think I'd abandon you, though you abandoned us?"

Was there a barb in that tone? I wanted to see his face, but with the mask limiting my sight, I couldn't politely turn my head far enough.

"And the others?"

"Antoine has escorted Daphné and Claire back."

"I apologize," I murmured. "You should not have forsaken Daphné on my account."

"Indeed," he said. "I shall pay for that later." But the sharpness had gone from his voice, replaced by the laconic drawl I'd come to know him for.

I relaxed momentarily, but then began to chafe at the pace of his walk. With my arm through his, I could not take larger steps. His bent elbow was the shepherd's crook that kept me from running free.

Observe, then, I thought to myself. *Let this be your first subject from which to learn the court's tongue.*

I was exhausted from walking—not too quickly, but too slowly—by the time Michel delivered me back to the apartment. All I wanted was to slip off my damnable shoes and unlace my stays, but Michel would not leave. My newly learned decorum dictated that by sitting I would invite him to do likewise, and so we stood, his elbow upon the fireplace mantel, my hips resting against the back of the chaise to at least remove some weight from my throbbing feet.

Claire was not here, though she had returned earlier. And nor was her mother.

"May I pour you a glass of rossolis?" Michel asked at last, gesturing with his lace-cuffed hand to the decanters on the sideboard.

Of course. He had been waiting for me to offer. If it had been Henri, I mused, he would already have his boots off and be drinking from the bottle.

I gave up. The language of gestures and expectations was still beyond me. "Help yourself," I said, abandoning decorum. "These stays are murderous, and I need to change." I kicked off my shoes and left them where they were, along with Michel and the decanter.

The stays were laced in the back, and I couldn't reach them without removing my stomacher, which entailed taking off my jacket and sleeves. I was only on the first of these when there was a scratch at the door.

I exhaled, none too quietly. "Entrez."

Michel came in, my slippers in hand. "May I be of assistance? Your maid seems absent."

"Claire is hardly my maid, and that seems hardly appropriate."

"Tt. I'm your brother, my dear. What are siblings for if not to lend aid?"

I glared at him. "Sir, I have four sisters and a brother. You are none of them. And they have never needed to help me undress."

"Would that we all wore the simple garb of the countryside," he said with a sad shake of his head. I didn't believe him for an instant—I simply could not imagine Michel de Foix in anything but his peacock finery.

"You are a poor liar," I said as he undid the ribbons at the back of my sleeves and carefully slid one, then the other, off and laid them on the bed. Resigned, I handed him the hook so he could undo the stomacher while I untied the points of my overskirt. At last the wretched laces of the stays were revealed. I slumped in relief once they were loosened, and reached for a robe.

"Thank you for your help … brother."

"The pleasure was all mine, sister dear," he said, kissing me fraternally on both cheeks. "And now," he said, "the hour grows late, and I must leave."

At last, I thought.

"You have become a creature of the court remarkably well," he continued. "If Claire had not told me of your humble beginnings, I would not have credited the story as true. I have stayed as long as I feasibly can, but can delay it no longer, and you have something I need."

I was truly puzzled now.

"The letter opener, Toinette."

I blinked, hoping my honest surprise would cover my lie. "I don't know what you're talking about, m'sieur. And where are you going?"

He ignored the question. "Come, now. Do you think that Henri, buffoon though he is, would not notice its absence? He accused me of taking it. And while I'm clever, I'm not clever enough to steal an object I didn't know he had. Last I had heard, it was in Sauvegarde's keeping. Henri doesn't have a clue it was you. But having eliminated Mathilde, Claire, and the Countess herself, I have determined it could *only* be you. Now, if you would be so kind as to hand it over, I will see it reaches its rightful owner."

"And that would be …?" I asked

"Why, His Majesty, of course. Charles of England."

The chamber seemed suddenly cramped, the space between myself and Michel too small for air. I could feel the criss-crossed strands of political intrigue tighten around me like the corset, squeezing the breath from me. Less than a year ago I had been a shepherdess from St Geneviève — now I held the possessions of kings. Why had I taken it in the first place? It was nothing but trouble, and why shouldn't Michel have it? I owed Henri nothing, for had he not taken the knife from Sauvegarde? Who was I to determine who lied, who told the truth, and who had any right to the object? And why should I risk myself over it? I looked at Michel with fresh eyes, conscious for the first time of the sword he wore at his hip, of how, though he was no taller than I, his shoulders stretched the satin of his coat. Should I be afraid? I couldn't tell.

"I know nothing of it," I said again. "How would I come into something belonging to the English king?"

Surely, I thought, he could see the lie on my face. But I calmed my breath and held back my fear. The worst thing you can do when facing a wolf or mad dog is cower or run, so I drew myself up to my full height and looked as haughty and imposing as a shepherdess in borrowed dress — that is to say, a sheep in wolf's clothing — may.

He slumped. "Damn. I didn't think so, but it was worth the try."

The shock of him giving up so easily nearly buckled my knees with relief. I eased myself onto the edge of the bed as calmly as I might. I felt the invisible web loosen around me, and breath came at last.

He picked up my hand and kissed it, not as a brother but as a courtier. "My apologies, mademoiselle, for the baseless accusation. I had to be sure."

A seed of scepticism bloomed in the depths of my relief. If he could not tell I was lying, how could I tell whether he was? And if he still suspected me, was this a different course to get me off guard? Should I be forgiving or affronted? I chose a path between.

"I am puzzled, m'sieur, and I confess somewhat hurt, that you should take me for a thief. I am a country lass, it's true, but an honest one." I shocked myself with how easily that lie rolled from my lips.

His blue eyes were all innocence and apology once more, and he hadn't yet let go of my hand. "It was unforgivable of me to accuse you so. I am so accustomed to the deceits of court, I see them in every face. It is my shame to have imagined it in a creature so pure as you."

This was too much. I withdrew my hand. "Sir, you've insulted my character already this evening, do not insult my intelligence with sideways flattery. Speak plainly. What is the significance of this letter opener, and why did you suspect me of taking it?"

He shook his head. "I am sorry, mademoiselle, but truly, the less you know of it the better."

"No, that will not do," I insisted. "You let slip the name of Sauvegarde, and that vile man is someone against whom I hold a mighty grudge. Are you his friend?"

"Sauvegarde is a friend to himself alone. Even the band of ruffians he keeps near him is held by money, not love. He is a mercenary himself, of sorts, but his wages come in favours and titles rather than coin. He was paid with a rather significant scrap of land across the channel for his latest task, but he was intercepted before he could complete it, and the tool he would have used was stolen."

"This letter opener? His task was to read mail?"

"A letter opener can open a man's—or woman's—throat as easily as it can a letter."

I felt my skin prickle between my breasts, where the weapon nestled, sewn to the central stay. I had stitched it in the day after I had taken it from Henri. "But Sauvegarde has any number of weapons he is not shy to use. Why should the loss of that one stop him?"

"Those weapons are his. This one is easily identifiable as someone else's."

If I hadn't been sitting already, I may have foundered, loosened stays or not. The letter opener glowed with an imagined heat, and I willed myself to neither touch nor glance down at my chest. "Where do you go now, Chevalier?" I asked.

"Better you not know, my dear."

"And when I am asked the whereabouts of my brother?

"Tell them I have returned to our estate."

"Will we see you again?"

"God willing." He smiled. "I have never stayed long from the court. Its attractions are too fine."

I stood, retrieved a shawl from the dressing table, and wrapped it around my shoulders.

"In that case, I bid you au'voir, but not adieu," I said. "I wish you luck in finding your letter opener."

I wondered if I was making an error, not finding out more from him while I had the chance. Perhaps it would be better to simply hand the perilous item over to him. But I didn't know whom I should trust in this, and recalled once more who had given the poisoned pomander to Marie-Claire.

I waited till evening, when Mathilde and Claire had returned and gone again to fetch our dinner from the kitchens. Reaching down my front with a seam ripper, I opened the central stay pocket and drew out the letter opener. It had seemed the only place safe from Marie-Claire's nosy fingers, which found their way into all the dressers, chests, and drawers in our apartment. I knew this from the way my own personal supply of lavender cream continued to diminish, no matter which cachette I moved it to. Since the only time I wasn't wearing my stays was when I was in the room with them, my bodice remained the safest place to keep the object.

I turned it over in my hands, wondering at this small simple thing that Henri, Sauvegarde, the minister, Madame, and the King all seemed to want, even so much as to kill for. Why?

It was beautiful, true, with the gold-inlay handle and silver blade. Pure silver too, I guessed by the heavy warmth of it. I took a handkerchief and some ash from the hearth and rubbed the tarnish off, admiring the milky sheen. Silver indeed. I smiled. A year ago, I would not have been able to tell silver from lead. I finished polishing the blade and went to work on the handle, using my fingernail behind the linen to clean the cracks of the filigree. As I did so, the circular blazon of entwined L's twisted, shifted, and clicked, turning ninety degrees to the handle.

I felt the handle loosen and separate. I pulled gently, worried that I had broken it. The handle came away, drawing with it the tang from inside the silver blade. But it wasn't a tang. It was a blade within a blade: thin, narrow, and most definitely steel. It was so thin, in fact, that it was more a needle than a knife at the tip. And it was coated with something white and sticky.

It was fortunate that I had had months of study with Dr Ahmed. Instead of wiping the blade with my kerchief as I might have, I snapped it back into its sheath. I twisted the L's back into place, locking the device, and shuddered to think I had been carrying a poisoned needle between my breasts. And yet where else was it to go? Did Henri know its true nature when he bound it with thread to the inside of his belt? Or Sauvegarde, when he carried it in the satchel Henri had rifled that night at the inn? And if it truly belonged to either our king or England's, what use did Their Majesties have for a poisoned stiletto?

I slid the letter opener back into the stay pocket with a shudder, trusting the silver scabbard to continue to protect me, and sewed it shut. But I used only two stitches. In case I needed it in a hurry.

Dr Ahmed turned the knife over in his hands and looked at me with curiosity. "No, mademoiselle, I do not recognize it. Should I?"

I quivered a little inside, both in relief and fear, but kept my face calm as I took the letter knife back. I sprang the mechanism, laid the letter opener down on the piece of parchment I had placed on Ahmed's work table, and drew the two halves apart.

He bent over, swooping like a hawk, his long nose hovering dangerously close to the suspect item. When he straightened, his soft eyes had hardened. "Why do you have a poisoned needle, Antoinette?"

"It's not mine. Is it arsenic?" I asked.

"You don't know?"

"It has no odour that I can detect. It could be monkshood. I'd like to assay it."

"Your nose, tiny though it is, is far better than mine. But yes, we can test it."

"Can you tell me who might have compounded it?"

He shook his head. "It's not an uncommon poison, as you know. La Voisin dealt in such, as did her acolytes. If there is anything unusual about it ... perhaps. Where did you get it? No, wait—I don't want to know." His look was stern. "I think you are a young and innocent girl, am I correct?"

"I am young, doctor, and innocent of wrongdoing—except for having taken this as a prank from someone I have no wish to harm. How can I return it to that person, knowing this is inside?"

He nodded. "Let us puzzle this, then, and I will leave it to your conscience as to what to do with what we find."

By the time Dr Ahmed and I had finished the assays, there was not a speck of the substance left inside or out of the letter opener. However, I soaked it in vinegar, washed it with lye, and polished its crevices with tufts of lambswool to be sure. And still it gave me a shiver down my spine when I slid it back into my bodice.

I confess I had been hoping for some magical insight from Ahmed's alchemical prowess that could tell us who had concocted the poison, but such powers were beyond him.

"Do you take our art for sorcery?" he asked.

I glowed briefly at the word 'our' but shook my head, deflated.

"However," he continued, "look at this." He slid a square of flat glass in front of the ocular stand and smeared it with a thin film of the diluted poison. "What do you see?"

"It looks like the clay we use for making pastes. But white, not red."

He nodded. "Most of the clay found here in Paris, and all the way south to the Occitanie, is red. Someone made this with clay from the north — the Pas de Calais, the low countries, or England."

"So we have only eliminated half of Europe." I sighed.

"It is a lot to eliminate. More specifically, it eliminates the disciples of La Voisin."

"So is there a new poisoner in court? A northern one?"

"Perhaps. But instead of looking for a poisoner, perhaps one might look for the likely target."

"Henri," I ventured as the man sprawled his giant form across the settee, dropping dried mud from his boots on the damask upholstery. "The night we met, you stole a letter knife from Sauvegarde."

The eyes that had just closed snapped open and peered at me. "Stole? No, no, ma petite. Sauvegarde was the thief. I reclaimed it from him."

"What is so important about a letter opener that Sauvegarde was willing to pursue and attempt to kidnap me to retrieve it?"

I poured another generous dram of brandy into his empty glass. He downed it — his fourth so far.

"Well, it's a pretty piece of metalwork, clearly belonging to His Majesty. I am quite sure he wants it back — and will pay for it. Why are you asking?"

"Michel came and asked to borrow a letter opener," I lied. "When I lent him Madame's, he looked … disappointed. It reminded me of the one you had. Have you not given it back to His Majesty?"

We stared at one another, and I saw wheels of suspicion grinding behind Henri's drink-blurred eyes.

"No. There are others who will pay more."

"More than a king? And have you sold it to them?"

"I didn't say they wanted to own it. Some people pay for things to disappear."

"But you haven't thrown it in a river."

"That would be a waste. Someone may pay yet more for it to resurface. Why do you want to know, mademoiselle?"

Michel was safely gone from Versailles, and Henri's ire seldom lasted long, so I put forth a morsel of the truth. With a wounded air, I said, "Michel thought *I* had it. He accused me of stealing it from you."

"A sweet fillette like you?" Henri waved a dismissive hand, but I could see his mind was elsewhere, chasing Michel. I felt a momentary wave of guilt for setting these two men against one another, but I reminded myself that neither had been honest with me.

That was all I got from Henri, but it was more than nothing. Why did a poisoned needle bear the King's emblem? If the King wanted to poison someone, he would order another to do it, and would certainly not use a weapon emblazoned with his sigil—unless it had been a gift, with the goal of shifting the blame of murder. No one would turn down a gift from the King. Even if they had knowledge of its deadly innards.

The knife felt ever more dangerous to carry, devoid of poison though it now was. It also seemed impossible to question Henri any further without divulging that I now held it. I was still angry with Henri, but part of me didn't want him to carry the dangerous item either.

I committed every detail of the letter opener to memory, both its outward aspect and the hidden stiletto, and spent half my attention throughout every day looking for clues to its origin or identity. There was no maker's mark on the steel, which led me to think it had been commissioned for murder from the start. Otherwise who would not sign such beautiful handiwork? In every drawing room I visited, I cast a sideways eye at anything made of metal—not just letter knives and cutlery, but clocks and firedogs, silver plate and coffrets, even the filigreed frames of miniature portraits.

At last, as I sat reading from Rabelais to Liselotte, I stumbled upon a word.

"I do not know what this means, Madame."

She took the book from me, held it at arm's length, and peered down her nose at the text. She shook her head. "Damn these failing eyes," she said and fumbled in her reticule, pulling out a small gold-filigreed disc. She pressed the centre and twisted with her thumb—a motion by now familiar to me—and a perfect round glass in a gold loop sprang from the casing.

She held it above the page. "Ah, viniculture. It is an unnecessarily grand word for the growing of grapes." She snapped the lens back into its case and handed me the book once more.

"May … may I see your glass, Madame?" I asked, precociously holding out my hand.

"Toinette, you are too young for this. I hope your eyes are not failing already?"

"No, Madame—I have just never seen one so beautiful," I said, turning the finely crafted case in my hands." Nor so like my letter opener, I thought. The filigree pattern was not at all similar to the knife's, but the round emblem, this one with the initials 'P + E', was a near twin to the release catch on the letter opener. I pressed and twisted with my thumb, and the innocent and helpful magnifying glass hinged out of its case with the same soft click I had come to know so well.

"Wherever did you acquire it?"

"It was a wedding gift from the Chevalier de Lorraine. He is a disgusting man, but he knows the best craftsmen."

This felt like news indeed, though all I had found out was that the Duc d'Orleans's lover had once purchased a gift from the same craftsman who had made the letter opener.

"Henri," I asked that evening, "who is it who has paid you to have the letter opener disappear?"

We were sitting across the chequer table from each other.

"Toinette, why would you want to know such a thing?"

"Because if you don't tell me, I shall send a message to the Chevalier de Lorraine that you have it."

His eyebrows shot up momentarily, then lowered onto his scowl like thick black thunderclouds. "Mademoiselle, the Chevalier is possibly the most dangerous man at court, even in exile as he is now. Do not trifle with him."

"Who, then?" I insisted.

He sighed and sat back in the delicate chair, making it creak alarmingly.

"Monsieur."

The King's brother. "So he is protecting his lover. From what? Or whom?"

"Why do you think the opener belongs to him?"

"I did not say that. But you have confirmed it. Does Sauvegarde work for Monsieur or for the Chevalier?"

"Toinette, it is not good for you to know such things."

"But I do." I leaned over the table, matching his scowl with my glare. "Thanks to you. You used me as a decoy in the tavern on the road."

"I did." He nodded and looked down at his thick hands. "And then thought the worse of myself for it. I tried to make amends. I rescued you from them; I brought you to Catrin. Let this go, Toinette. If I tell you more, I will be endangering you all over again."

"At least this time it is my choice. Who did the Chevalier have killed with that knife?"

"Minette," came a voice from behind me. Madame stood in the doorway. To Henri she said, "Tell her. She deserves to know, for she has found the proof we need."

§

The Shepherdess *will continue in* Pulp Literature *Issue 34, Spring 2022.*

THE PIANIST WHO SERENADED THE MERMAIDS WITH CHOPIN'S NOCTURNE IN E MINOR

Tais Teng

Tais Teng *is a Dutch writer and illustrator with some hundred and twenty novels and more pictures than he can count. If he isn't writing or painting, he likes to carve eerie gargoyles from sandstone.*

The Pianist Who Serenaded the Mermaids with Chopin's Nocturne in E Minor

All day long the piano stood in the middle of the shifting sands, its plastic cover flapping in the breeze. At dusk, when the sky was as green as a beetle shield, Gerald emerged from his beachcomber's hut. The sea was quiet, the surfers long gone. Gerald lifted the cover, cracked his knuckles, and began to play.

Soon the first head emerged from the surf, bobbing like a fisherman's float. Such shining eyes, reflecting the last of sunlight. The mermaids smiled but took care not to bare their sharp teeth or lick their rosy lips with their forked tongues.

"Gerald!" the mermaids called out. "Come to us. Play in Ran's palace on the wide sandy bottom where the dance halls are lit by phosphorescent deep-sea fishes."

Gerald shook his head.

"I am waiting for one of your sisters. Sweet Maryanne who walked from the waves, on two human legs, when I played my piano. We spent a single night together in my hut. But in the morning she was gone, her mother-of-pearl comb left as a token of her love and a promise that she would return."

"O, you foolish mortal!" one of the mermaids said. "We are granted only a single day on shore to walk on shapely legs. At sunrise we pay the price, turning into foam and spindrift, with only a mother-of-pearl comb left behind."

But Gerald did not believe her and played on.

THE ARTISTS

Tais Teng

Cover artist, The Pianist Who Serenaded the Mermaids with Chopin's Nocturne in E Minor

This is Tais Teng's sixth cover for *Pup Literature*. When he paints, a story often pops up, telling him what the painting is about. *The Pianist* began with an HDR picture of an abandoned piano. Tais made the piano a lot grungier and added the beach ambiance. The story, by asking who would be playing the piano on a deserted beach, was easy to write. You can read more of Tais's illustrated stories at deviantart.com/taisteng/gallery/50687452/illustrated-stories.

Tais Teng's covers are a combination of digital paintings, HDR photographs, and fractals. In short, he uses whatever works. When he started as an artist, there were no computers, so he still uses paintbrush and pencil. His novel *Phaedra: Alastor 824*, set in the universe of Jack Vance, was recently published by Spatterlight Press.

Matthew Nielsen

Artist, 'Houses'

Matthew Nielsen (aka Nuclear Jackal) is a comic artist currently working on *Toni & Aberdeen*, a graphic novel about two time travellers living in an empty 2003 Vancouver. He has illustrated Monstercat's *8 Year Anniversary* comic and David Edwards's *The Cold and Actual Sky* and *Forever the Star Finder*. His own comics have appeared in *BANG! Magazine*, *Sequential Magazine*, and two Cloudscape Comics anthologies (plus a zine about bees). He has also created merchandise artwork for both Military History Visualized and Military Aviation History. His story, 'The Endless Drop', inked by Minna Hakkola, appeared in Issue 22, Spring 2019, of *Pulp Literature*.

Matthew was raised by a Danish father and a Canadian mother in a Welsh port town. He was identified with special needs from a young age and eventually diagnosed with Asperger's Syndrome at age eleven. He was expelled from secondary school at twelve, then went to a school for violent teenagers. He was told he was the first person educated there to pass a national exam, and went on to college and then university, where he graduated with a degree in Illustration. 'Houses' is inspired by the many moves in Matthew's own life. Part one appears in *Pulp Literature* Issue 31, Summer 2021. Matthew now lives in Canada, and as of this writing has just moved house again.

Mel Anastasiou
In-house illustrator

Mel Anastasiou loves drawing for *Pulp Literature* because she loves the stories she illustrates. She draws in black and white, working from imagination and inspired by details from Renaissance compositions. You can find illustrations, writing tips, and news about her books and novellas at melanastasiou.wordpress.com, and see more of her artwork on Facebook at Bird and Branch Artwork.

HALL OF FAME

These are the heroes — the Patrons and Pulp Literati whose monthly support helped bring you this issue. Please lift your glasses and give them a rousing cheer!

The Shareholders
Rapscallion

The Brewers
Robin McGillveray
A Bursewicz

The Landlords
Isabel Cushey
Dana Tye Rally

The Innkeepers
Ada Maria Soto
Margot Landels
Ev Bishop
Shannon Saunders
Roger & Anne Anastasiou
Kevin Harris
Gillian Gardiner
Megan Shaw
Susan Jackson
Meghan Dahl

The Cicerones
Elsa Carruthers

The Bartenders
Alana Krider
Richard Gropp
Ron Graves

Kristen Mah
Robert Bose
Victoria McAuley
Dave Wayne
Scott F Gray
Michelle Balfour
Abigail Bruce
Vernice Dietra Malik
Katriona Greenmoor
AD Bane
KT Wagner
Michael Weckworth
Deepthi Atukorala
Margot Spronk
Margaret Elliott
Peter Halasz
Bjarne Hansen
Leny Wagner
Kain Stewart
Chris Olee
kc dyer
Kimberley Aslett
Jan Fagan
Ken Oakes
Brighton Hugg
Alexa Benzaid-
Williams
Bryan Moose
Maureen Cooke

Lorna Keach
Katja Rammer

The Regulars
CC Humphreys
Marta Salek
Rina Piccolo
Emily Lonie
Jenny Blackford
Jain Cairns
Akemi Art
BC
Meredith Frazier
Catherine Levinson
Vera
Charity Tahmaseb
Alexander Langer
Marilyn Holt
Risa Wolf
Barbara Pengelly
David Perlmutter
Christine McCullough
Ishbel Newstead

The Clientele
Ray Hsu
Melissa Hudson

If you would like to join the ranks of these worthies, you can become a patron on Patreon at patreon.com/pulplit or join the Pulp Literati through our website at pulpliterature.com/join-pulp-literati/.

Have you heard?

Pulp Literature has a podcast!

Our podcast **The Pulp Lit Pulpit** is available on Podbean. The episodes are filled with editor advice, exclusive author interviews, and serialized story-time instalments from *Allaigna's Song: Overture* and *Stella Ryman and the Fairmount Manor Mysteries*.

Each episode has a limited lifespan of about eight to twelve weeks, after which it's gone! The episodes are available for download so you can save them for when you want to hear them most. **Find the latest episodes here:** pulpliterature.podbean.com

https://pulpliterature.com   @pulpliteraturepress

MARKETPLACE

Books

Advent *by Michael Kamakana* • We thought we knew what the aliens wanted. Think again. • pulpliterature.com/advent

Allaigna's Song: Chorale *by JM Landels* • The long-awaited conclusion to the bestselling *Allaigna's Song* trilogy. • pulpliterature.com/allaignas-song

The Extra: A Monument Studios Mystery *by Mel Anastasiou* • Extra Frankie Ray gets her big break on the Silver Screen, until Murder steals the scene. pulpliterature.com/the-extra

The Labours of Mrs Stella Ryman: Further Fairmount Mysteries *by Mel Anastasiou* • Trapped in a down-at-the-heels care home. You'd be cranky too. • pulpliterature.com/stella-ryman-and-the-fairmount-manor-mysteries

What the Wind Brings *by Matthew Hughes* • Winner of the 2020 Endeavour Award • pulpliterature.com/product-category/novels/matthew-hughes

The Writer's Boon Companion *by Mel Anastasiou* • Thirty Days Towards an Extraordinary Volume • pulpliterature.com/subscribe/the-bookstore

Bookstores

Book Warehouse • 632 Broadway W, Vancouver, BC V5Z 1G1 • 604-872-5711 bookwarehouse.ca

Myth Hawker Travelling Bookstore • Canadian authors • Canadian content • small and independent press • mythhawker.ca

Phoenix On Bowen • 992 Dorman Rd, Bowen Island, BC V0N 1G0 • 604-947-2793

Village Books & Coffee House • 130-12031 First Ave, Richmond, BC V7E 3M1 • 604-272-6601 • villagebooks@shaw.ca

Western Sky Books • 2132-2850 Shaughnessy St, Port Coquitlam, BC V3C 6K5 • 604-461-5602 • store.westernskybooks.com

White Dwarf / Dead Write Books • 3715 10th Ave W, Vancouver, BC V6R 2G5 • 604-228-8223 • whitedwarf@deadwrite.com

Conferences and Events

Surrey International Writers' Conference 22–24 October 2021 • Virtual Event • siwc.ca

Word on the Lake • May 2022 • Salmon Arm, BC • wordonthelakewritersfestival.com

Creative Ink Festival • May 2022 Burnaby, BC • creativeinkfestival.com

When Words Collide • August 2022 Calgary, AB • whenwordscollide.org

Wine Country Writers' Festival September 2022 • Penticton, BC winecountrywritersfestival.ca

GEIST
Keep it weird.
Subscribe today!
go to geist.com/subscribe
or call 1-888-GEIST-EH
LOST CITY
FACT + FICTION ◦ NORTH of AMERICA

on spec
the canadian magazine of the fantastic
Expect the unexpected.
www.onspec.ca

Do you have a **story to tell?**
We can help!

Dreamers is dedicated to heartfelt writing. Visit our site for:

- Therapeutic Writing
- Poems & Stories
- Content Marketing
- Creative Nonfiction
- Writing Workshops
- Contests & Anthologies
- Residencies & Retreats
- ...and so much more!

www.DreamersWriting.com

DREAMERS
CREATIVE WRITING

COMING SOON FROM PULP LITERATURE PRESS
Allaigna's Song: Chorale
JM LANDELS
THE MAGNIFICENT FINALE OF THE BESTSELLING ALLAIGNA'S SONG TRILOGY
Allaigna's Song
Overture
AMAZON #1 BESTSELLER
JM Landels
Allaigna's Song
Aria
JM Landels
pulpliterature.com

CONTESTS

Pulp Literature runs four annual contests for poetry, flash fiction, and short stories. For contest guidelines, prizes, and entry fees, see pulpliterature.com/contests.

The Bumblebee Flash Fiction Contest
Contest opens: 1 January 2022
Deadline: 15 February 2022
Winner notified: 15 March 2022
Winner published: Issue 35, Summer 2022
Prize: $300

The Magpie Award for Poetry
Contest opens: 1 March 2022
Deadline: 15 April 2022
Winner notified: 15 May 2022
Winner published: Issue 36, Autumn 2022
Prize: $500

The Hummingbird Flash Fiction Prize
Contest opens: 1 May 2022
Deadline: 15 June 2022
Winner notified: 15 July 2022
Winner published: Issue 37, Winter 2023
Prize: $300

The Raven Short Story Contest

Contest opens: 1 September 2022

Deadline: 15 October 2022

Winner notified: 15 November 2022

Winner published: Issue 38, Spring 2023

Prize: $300

$\mathcal{B}$ecome a Patron of Pulp Literature

By supporting *Pulp Literature* on Patreon with $2 or more per month, you will be laying the foundation for a secure future for the magazine, as well as ensuring that you never miss an issue! Your subscription includes four big issues of short stories, novellas, poetry, comics, and novel excerpts, delivered to your door or electronic mailbox each year. **Find us at patreon.com/pulplit**

If you prefer to subscribe through our website, go to pulpliterature.com/subscribe.

Or you can send a cheque with the form below to
Subscriptions, Pulp Literature Press, 21955 16 Ave, Langley BC, V2Z 1K5, Canada

Don't miss an issue!

- ☐ **Send me 2 years (8 issues) at the special rate of $90** (save $30)*
- ☐ **Send me 1 year (4 issues) for $50** (save $10)*
- ☐ **Send me 2 years of digital issues for $30** (save $9.92)
- ☐ **Send me 1 year of digital issues for $17.50** (save $2.47)

Name: ____

Address: ____

City: _____________________________ Prov. / State: _________

Postal code: ____________ Country: _______________________

Email: ____

- ☐ **Payment enclosed**
- ☐ **Bill me**
- ☐ **New**
- ☐ **Renewal**

Make cheques payable in Canadian funds to Pulp Literature Press. Include email address for digital editions and Paypal billing, or subscribe at www.pulpliterature.com.

*for postage outside Canada add $20 per year in North America or $36 per year overseas.